DODGING FATE 2

EXTRA FATEFUL, UBER DODGY

ZEN DIPIETRO

ISBN: 978-1-943931-29-3 (print)

Cover Art by Dyana Wangsa

Published in the United States of America by Parallel Worlds Press

ATTACK OF THE BLAGROOKS: A DODGING FATE HOLIDAY SPECTACULAR

1

THE HOLIDAYS ARE COMING. Are there four worse words in all the known universe?

If it were all about the joy and the togetherness, that would be dandy. I'm all *about* joy and togetherness.

But no. What the holiday season actually means is that a guy has to run around, searching for the perfect gifts for those he loves. If he fails to perfectly condense his entire relationship with someone down into one material object that he can wrap up in shiny paper and top with a bow, he will have ruined the entire holiday and possibly his relationship.

It's a lot to live up to, and frankly, I'm not built for that kind of stress.

I'm not someone who shines in emotionally fraught situations. I would absolutely freaking love to be the guy who has the answers, knows what to do, and springs into action. The kind who saves busloads full of children and can make a woman stop crying with a few witty words. You know, the hero type.

That's just not me. I'm the kind of guy who arrives on a planet with six others and is somehow the only one who walks by an eyeball-high flower that sprays deadly poison just as he's inhaling for a big sneeze.

Or maybe it's a people-eating plant. But never mind the botany. That's just a means to an end. The fact is, if there's an unlikely scenario that will probably lead to death, that's what happens to a redshirt like me.

Every year, the holidays roll around and I start to think of all the people I won't be celebrating with. All those dead Kenny relatives of Christmases past. I don't have visions of sugarplums when I sleep. I have nightmares about yeti-gators, fatal rutabaga missions, and those darn metal teeth at the top and bottom of escalators.

I really hate those things. They always seem poised to catch my toes and pull me in, like a meat grinder.

So, yeah. The holidays are a particularly tense time for me. I've been having nightmares, actually.

There's this particularly disturbing recurring dream that's plaguing me. In it, Greta keeps insisting her drink glass is empty. When I look inside, it's a black hole with a yeti-gator in the middle, trying to suck me in.

I'm having that dream again, right now.

Dammit.

I wake up, rubbing my eyes, blinking away the disturbing images. Then I become aware of a tickling sensation at the side of my neck.

It was probably the thing that woke me up.

I open my eyes and groan. I'm glad to break free of the dream, but not thrilled about the reason.

"Nana, you've got to stop trying to assimilate me. You don't have the right tools or equipment, and you know I don't want to become a cyborg."

Nana sits up straight, looking stricken. "Oh, dear, was I doing that again? I came in to collect your laundry to send it out for you, and the next thing I knew, you were telling me to stop assimilating you. I'm sorry, Charlie. Again."

I give her metal hand a squeeze. "It's okay. But please, stop breaking in here, for any purpose. I can send out my own laundry, and although waking up to a cyborg trying to assimilate me is no longer a shocker for me, it still freaks me the hell out."

"Just as it should, dear." Nana pats my cheek and straightens from her creepy, hovering-over-me position. "By the way, I still need your Christmas list."

In accordance with tradition, I mentally scream the cry of the damned. There is no winning this battle. A list of desired gifts will be required, as per the yearly protocol, in strict adherence with the gift-giving ritual.

Knowing an argument is pointless and that I'm effectively struggling while standing in a pit of quicksand, nonetheless I say, "You don't have to spend any money on me, Nana. I know your finances are tight due to the cyborg union cutting your allowance. Oh, and don't forget, we're celebrating the universal holidays, not just Christmas. So we can focus on that instead of the presents."

Most planets have some sort of celebration going on in the December or January part of the year. Since we live aboard the *Second Chance*, zooming from system to system, we're embracing a new-wave sort of celebration combination that includes a bunch of holidays all at once. It's a shame that nearly half of them involve gift giving, but I figure at least it cuts down the gift-giving occasions to one multipurpose celebration.

It makes logical sense, and as a statistician, I dig that.

"I don't forget things, Charlie. My hard drive just got upgraded before we left Earth, and I remember absolutely everything." She smiles at me in a very grandmotherly way, with her one red, cybernetic eye glowing.

"That's great, Nana. Do you want to have breakfast with me at Pinky's?"

She makes a tsking sound. "Now, you know I don't have

breakfast at a bar. It's just not proper. I'll catch up with you later, but thanks for the invitation, all the same."

After she leaves, I change out of my pajamas. I don't take it personally that Nana tries to assimilate me, really. It's an instinct that was built into her with her own assimilation. If she had access to any power tools, I'd be concerned, but until then, I'm determined to see this as an amusing personality quirk. Like Pinky's love for pranks and Greta's gross eating habits.

Ah, Greta. Lovely, golden Greta.

She, Pinky, and I have agreed to teach one another about our holiday celebrations. In this way, we can learn about each other, become more cosmopolitan—because no one likes a sectarian rube—and help each other celebrate.

Most importantly, I'm going to get my chance to kiss Greta, thanks to the old teach-you-about-the-mistletoe-tradition-of-my-people cliché.

As far as my Christmas list goes, that's the only thing that's on it. I'll do whatever it takes to make my holiday miracle come true.

WHILE I DIG into a plate of biscuits and gravy, Greta decimates a muffin, reducing it to barely more than crumbs. Only once it is a deconstructed pile does she begin eating.

"I keep meaning to ask," I say in a carefully casual tone. "Why do you eat that way?"

Greta peers at me, puzzled. "What do you mean?"

I point at the former muffin, which looks like it's been reduced to rubble by a tiny, tiny bomb. "Why not just take bites of it? Why tear it up first?"

Pinky finishes mixing a drink and edges closer, leaning against the bar. Apparently, she wants to hear the answer, too.

Greta stares down at her plate. "You mean just mash my face against the whole thing and bite it?"

"Yeah. That's how my people do it," I tell her. "Muffins, apples, sandwiches. We just bite off the piece we want to chew."

"I've seen people doing that." She sounds doubtful. "Where I'm from, it's polite to only eat what you can fit into your mouth whole."

"It's weird, and you look weird doing it." Pinky is not one to waste time with tact. "Nobody else does that. Just you Garbdorians."

"Oh." Greta looks crestfallen. "I guess I should do it like everyone else, since I'm the Chance Fleet's brand ambassador. If you're sure it's really what most people do."

"Positive," I say.

"Nobody wants to watch you eat muffin-colored dirt," Pinky adds.

"Why didn't you say something before?" Greta asks.

Pinky pulls the rag off her shoulder and begins wiping the bar. "If I point out all the weird-ass things you two do, I'd never get anything else done. Besides, I've found that people rarely like to be told that they're strange. It's bad for business."

"It's not like she's paying," I point out. As the fleet's brand ambassador, Greta lives on the *Second Chance* entirely free. Pinky does, too, as the bartender. Of the three of us, I'm the only one who pays. I don't mind that distinction. I'm just glad my job as a statistician allows me to work from anywhere. It's a lucky break that allowed my life to become actually enjoyable.

No, not just enjoyable. Fun. Adventurous. Even exciting.

Such things are anathema to my people. And yet here I am, thanks to Greta's unique luck, and Pinky's unique...well, everything. As a pink, seven-foot-tall, Mebdarian mutant, there's no one in the entire universe to compare her to.

"I like Greta, though," Pinky assures us. "You too. And my understanding of friendship is that if you want people to stay friends, you don't point out all the things about them that are annoying."

She returns to mixing drinks. This early in the day, the bar isn't too busy, but the dining room does big business in breakfast cocktails.

Greta and I stare at each other, and I can tell that she feels the way I do. That Pinky just gave us both a ringing smackdown by explaining how much she has to rein herself in order to remain friends with us.

Wow. Apparently, what we've seen from her *is* her tactful mode.

I have no defense to this sudden revelation, other than to dig into my biscuits and gravy with renewed fervor, as if consuming this food is my sole purpose in life.

It's a bad defense, sure, but it's all I've got right now.

Greta seems to have lost her enthusiasm for her blueberry muffin, but doesn't quite know what to do with the remaining baked-good carnage, either.

In a burst of inspiration, I ask her, "Have you ever tried biscuits and gravy?"

Like a fool, I spoon up a bit of it—no, I'm not over my fork phobia yet, let's please not dwell on that—and extend it toward her.

As if she wants to take a bite of my half-eaten breakfast, from my pre-used spoon.

Stupid, stupid, stupid.

But miraculously, she leans forward and accepts the offering. She chews slowly, looking uncertain at first, then curious, then pleasantly surprised.

"That is not at all the most awful thing I've tasted!" she exclaims.

I'm not sure how to take this.

She notices my expression. "I mean, I'd try that."

Elation rushes over me, far out of proportion for the situation, but I don't care. I offered Greta something, she took it, and she liked it.

"Pinky," I call to my big friend's back, "could you order Greta some biscuits and gravy? In the spirit of the season, she's trying something new."

Greta beams at me. Her natural luminescence seems to increase at moments like this. I've read that a Garbdorian's emotional state can do that.

"Sure," Pinky calls back.

I half expect some witty retort, but it doesn't come. Maybe she's reining herself in.

Greta puts her napkin over her muffin dust, as if burying a dead thing. "How's your nana settling in?"

"She's adjusting to life aboard a starship. Some things she's taken to right away. Others are taking time." I don't mention her habit of trying to assimilate me. Some things should be kept within the family.

"It's only been a few days," Greta says, looking sympathetic. "I'm sure at her age, it takes time to adjust."

I finish off my breakfast and push the plate away. "You'd think so, but ever since she became a cyborg, she's surprisingly adaptable."

A porter arrives to whisk away yet another tray of drinks and Pinky returns to stand across the bar counter from us.

"Makes sense," she says thoughtfully. "Otherwise, how could she function? She's been through a lot of changes. I don't know what Nana Rose was like before, but she's A-OK with me. She's a great cook and a fantastic driver."

I say nothing and merely nod. Nana's cooking these days is inedible, and her driving is terrifying. Somehow, though, Pinky and Nana bonded almost immediately, and I haven't decided yet how I feel about that.

I mean, it's mostly good. I think. It's just that I haven't conquered my ingrained pessimism and the feeling that most things will somehow cause my untimely demise.

Some habits are hard to break.

I'm working on it, though. I'm making progress, right along with my ability to peacefully coexist with forks. These things take time.

"Has she ever been to Earth's International Space Station?" Greta asks.

"No," I answer. "She was never much for traveling before her assimilation. She's gotten much more adventurous since. Actually, I've never been there, either."

My people don't typically travel.

"Oh, you'll like it, I think," Greta says. "I've been there a couple of times. It used to be this place of scientific research for Earth, but now it's more of a museum for your whole solar system."

I look at her and wonder if I should verify the definition of "museum." There have been times when a word means something to her that is entirely different than what the word means to me. "You mean, like, a place you visit and look at things, but can't touch, and stuff's usually either really old or really expensive?"

She gives me an odd look. "Yeah. A museum."

I nod agreeably. "Okay. Sounds cool."

Very, very few deaths ever occur at museums.

"I'll show you and your nana around," Greta says. "I might not be able to spend all day, because I need to memorize my lines for my movie role, but we should be able to get in a few hours of sightseeing, anyhow."

Pinky has bent down and is rummaging inside a cabinet.

I call to her, "Hey, Pinky, do you want to check out the space station with Nana, Greta, and me?"

Pinky's forehead appears above the bar top, immediately followed by her eyes, like a frog surfacing in a pond. Startled, I grasp the edge of the bar to keep my balance.

She stands all the way up. "Museums aren't my thing, most of the time. I'm not much for fawning over some piece of crap because it's supposed to be historically significant. But since

Nana Rose is going, I'll check it out. With her along, it could be fun."

A porter arrives with Greta's food, and she scoops some up with a spoon. In an unspoken kindness toward me, Pinky doesn't stock forks in her bar.

I wonder, though, if I've made a mistake by inviting Pinky to a museum. "Fun" is a more of an extreme sport for her than a pleasant passing of time.

But it's too late now. I invited and she accepted, and now we're all going to have some sort of time on the International Space Station.

I can only hope for an uneventful day.

"I DON'T GET IT." Nana stares at a cartoonish neo-Schrödingerian portrait.

"It's a commentary on how space travel has made life more convenient, and yet more complicated," Greta explains. "It represents duality and ambiguity."

Nana continues to stare. "It's a cat on a flying saucer. And a drunk monkey could have done a better job of drawing it."

So far, Nana has not been impressed with the museum. She's pooh-poohed paintings, scoffed at sculptures, and downright dissed drawings.

To be honest, for the most part, I agree with her. Maybe art just isn't something the Kenny clan can appreciate. I'd much rather look at my Renard robot-western paintings than the strange mélange of display pieces I've seen here. Robot-westerns might not be high art that's worthy of a museum, but it's what speaks to me.

Greta seems a little disappointed that we aren't enjoying ourselves more. Pinky got bored and wandered off some time ago while Nana and I have dutifully followed our intrepid tour guide.

We stop in front of a collection of painted vases. Greta sighs. "You two aren't having any fun, are you?"

I try to form an artful reply that will confirm our boredom while tempering it with something positive that won't hurt her feelings.

Nana speaks before I can. "The last time I had such a crappy time, I was having my eyeball bored out by a cyborg."

So much for artful and positive.

Greta looks stricken. "Oh, my goodness! Well, let's find something else to do. Maybe you'd like to see the history of the station? There's a lot of old technology on display."

Nana perks up. "That could be interesting."

Back when she was purely human, Nana was not a fan of technology. I once caught her repeatedly poking a refrigerator door, expecting it to open itself, and getting increasingly frustrated that it wouldn't oblige. It was strange because spring-loaded refrigerators have never been a thing.

Now, though, it seems she has a great appreciation for technology. As we walk along, viewing a portion of the hull of the very first International Space Station and other historic Earth treasures, Nana avidly reads every word on the displays and listens to every audio clip.

I become increasingly suspicious. It's almost as if she's collecting information, as an advance reconnaissance scout would.

"Nana," I ask, "are you going to report on all this to the cyborgs?"

She blinks at me. "Of course. Union rules. All members must upload all information regarding technology. Even obsolete tech."

"Right." I want to edge away, but don't want to hurt her feelings. It's just strange sometimes that my cookie-baking, canasta-playing nana is subconsciously planning to overthrow Earth's government.

It's not her fault, but it's creepy and there's no handbook about how to deal with this sort of thing.

Greta also looks concerned, but she shakes her head and plasters on a cheery smile. "Should we go find Pinky? She said she'd meet us for lunch."

Nana's reply is immediate. "Yes! I love that big pink girl."

"She's a peach," I agree. It's something that Pinky frequently calls herself, and it amuses me to say it.

Greta grins at me, so I guess it amuses her, too.

Score.

Even in a large place, Pinky isn't hard to find. If her size isn't enough to do the trick, we can usually just follow the trail of startled or disgruntled people she's left in her wake.

We find her near the entrance of the art gallery, standing by a water fountain. She's posing with one hand on her hip and the other fist thrust forward, toward a growing group of onlookers. I'm not sure exactly what's happening.

"Three, two, one," Pinky announces in a booming voice, then she shifts so that she's shielding her eyes with one hand and pointing ahead and to her left with the other.

The crowd murmurs.

"What's going on?" I whisper to Nana and Greta. I don't know why I'm whispering, except there's a hushed sort of atmosphere, like at a library or a doctor's office.

They both shake their heads in puzzlement.

After a few minutes, Pinky says, "Three, two, one," and squats down, her arms straight out to her sides.

I've seen Pinky do a lot of unexpected things, but this is new.

After a full four minutes in her squat pose, she stands and announces in a booming voice, "We must be thirsty together."

She bows. The crowd, which has grown quite large, applauds for a full thirty seconds before beginning to disperse.

Pinky joins us, looking pleased with herself.

"What was that?" I ask.

"Performance art." She's clearly very happy about this.

"Okay. But, um, why?"

"Right place, right time," she says decisively. "I was bent over getting a drink from the fountain. As you know, it takes a lot to quench a Pinky-sized thirst. So as I'm drinking, I sense a crowd gathering. And I think to myself, now here's an interesting opportunity."

I'm almost afraid to ask, but she clearly wants me to or she wouldn't have paused in the middle of this story. There's nothing to do but pose the question. "What happened next?"

"I stood up and announced in a big voice, 'We are all thirsty. The universe is thirsty.' A couple of people nodded as if this meant something, so I struck my favorite dance pose." She demonstrates, standing with her legs apart, one hip thrust to the side, her left arm pointing down toward her foot and her right finger pointing at the one o'clock position.

Maybe one thirty. It's hard to be sure.

Onlookers notice the pose and begin drifting toward us again, perhaps thinking it's time for a second show.

"Yeah, great pose! You're such an awesome dancer. We should tell Nana about the time you two took me to the laundromat. Should we start walking to the restaurant? We don't want to miss our reservation." I take a few steps in that direction, hoping to move our little group onward.

Pinky looks at me. Crap. She's onto me. But then she nods. "Sure, let's walk and talk."

Whew.

"Anyway," she continues as we go, "the crowd is loving the dance pose, but I start thinking that standing still isn't all that entertaining. So I switch it up with a Statue of Liberty pose, you know, one hand holding a pretend torch and the other holding a pretend book. The crowd *loved* it. I wish I had my pointy hat so I could have really brought it home, but no matter. From there, I just made up some poses and let the folks make of them what they would. I'd say it was a very successful exhibit."

"What was that squatting one at the end?" Greta asks.

"To be honest," Pinky says, "I was running out of ideas. I'm kind of glad you guys came along when you did. I was trying to think of a big finish to wrap things up, like tearing the fountain clean off the wall or something. But I don't want to be banned from yet another place for that kind of thing, so it's lucky it was lunch time and I didn't need the big finish after all."

Yet another place?

How many places have banned Pinky for wanton destruction? Before I can ask, we've arrived at the restaurant and a waiter is eager to show us to our seats.

The place smells great and I'm perusing the menu when Pinky says, "Greta, you should have a sandwich and eat it bite by bite."

Greta freezes and her eyes widen like someone suddenly stricken with stage fright. "Oh. Today? Um..."

Though I'm far from the poster boy for trying new things, I decide to jump on this particular bandwagon. "Yeah, you should try it. It'll be great. Right, Nana?"

Nana looks up from her menu to blink at me. "What the hell do I care how she eats? I'm busy trying to find something to eat that won't gum up my servos."

I have no response to that.

Greta fills the awkward pause. "What the heck, I'll give it a try. The pastrami on rye looks good. What kind of meat is that?"

"That's kind of a long story," I say. "The short short version is that it's delicious and you should definitely try it."

Greta's looking at the menu. "Oh, and there's a picture of *cavalamitsi.* I'll have that."

"On Earth, we call it macaroni and cheese," I remind her gently. "But I'm sure it will be tasty."

"Ah, that's right. It's hard keeping all the food names straight sometimes." Greta laughs at herself.

I know she tries, though. As the Chance Fleet ambassador, she likes to be able to talk to people about their home worlds and suggest things to try at new destinations.

I love her natural inclination toward helpfulness. You just don't see a lot of that these days.

In solidarity, I choose a pastrami on rye and macaroni and cheese as well.

"Well, I don't want to be left out," Pinky says. She hands the server her menu. "I'll have what they're having."

"One more pastrami and macaroni," the waiter says agreeably, tapping the order into his telcoder.

"No," Pinky says this in a particularly *duh* tone of voice. "They're not sharing, are they? Two sandwiches. Two noodles. That's what I want. Don't shortchange me, bro."

She gives him a hard look.

"Certainly, ma'am," he says quickly. "My mistake."

Normally, I'd be concerned about someone taking a server to task before he delivers my food. Since nobody's stupid enough to serve Pinky a sneezer platter, I remain confident of my lunch's lack of contagious diseases.

"I'll have the entrée-sized clam chowder," Nana says. "But strain out the chunks. They gum up the works."

This, the server takes in stride. He must be accustomed to cyborg customers. "Anything else?"

"Extra crackers." Nana frowns thoughtfully. "You don't have any DW-101, do you?"

"We get a lot of requests for it," he says regretfully. "But no. Health codes prevent us from storing and serving commercial oil-based lubricants. I'm sorry."

"Not your fault," Nana assures him. "Laws never keep up with the needs of the people."

The waiter smiles. "That's true. I'll get this order in for you."

As we wait, Nana shifts her attention to Greta. "Charlie tells me you're going to film a movie while we're here? That's so exciting."

Greta nods, glowing with enthusiasm. "Yes, I did a tiny walk-on role for a film on Mars, and the director wanted me to be in his next movie, too. I was reluctant at first, but this sounded like a lot of fun. This is a named character and everything. It's going to take two whole days of shooting. And Pinky's going to be working on the second day, too. She came to check out the movie set on Mars, and the director said she was born for the movies."

"Of course she was! Look at her!" Nana points at Pinky. "She's the whole package."

"Thanks, Nana Rose." Pinky looks pleased.

Nana frowns, looking at Greta. "Not that you're not special, too, dear. You're quite pretty, and you sure do light up a room."

Greta laughs and waves a hand at Nana's worry over having hurt of feelings. "Oh, Pinky's definitely the eye-catching one. I look like anybody. Nothing special."

She means it, too. I love that about her. And while I know that most people see her as merely cute or pretty, I like that I'm the only one who can see how beautiful she really is. I'm like that ancient history dude who pulled a sword out of a lake because no one else could see it there.

"So what's your part in the movie, Pinky?" Nana asks.

"Oh, I'm this horrible monster."

This is news to me. I'm sad to learn that my magnificent friend is being reduced to a stereotype just because she's big.

"What?" Greta asks in confusion. "That's not the script I got."

"I sit around saying these super obvious things," Pinky says. "Then the other characters are all inspired and stuff, and go solve their own problems. Totally lame."

"Yes, you're the wise woman," Greta says. "The sage. Not a monster. You are the catalyst of enlightenment."

Pinky frowns, picking at her fingernails. "This must be a

different kind of movie, then. Where I come from, boring people who sit around saying smart stuff are monsters. The heroes are the ones that make exciting things happen, like buildings blowing up. Which I saw no mention of at all in this story."

"Oh." Greta presses her lips together. "Well I don't know if this makes it better or worse for you, but in this movie, your character is a sort of hero. There aren't any explosions, but your character is highly respected and revered."

"Huh. Okay. Well, I'll have to change my approach to this role, I guess." Pinky doesn't appear to be concerned.

For my part, I'm heartened and feeling kind of good about myself. Greta and Pinky are far more worldly than I am, and yet they still have some cultural mix-ups and misunderstandings. I am not as much of a sectarian rube as I thought.

Our food arrives, looking fantastic. The sandwiches are huge and arranged on plates with a garnish on top and some pickled vegetables on the side. For sandwiches, it's a pretty fancy setup. The pasta looks amazing too, all melty and steamy and wearing its own little green garnish on top.

Greta turns her plate, looking doubtful. "So I can't cut it?"

"Nope. All hands." Pinky hefts her sandwich to demonstrate. She takes a huge bite and chews happily.

"Okay..." Greta clamps her hands around the edges of the bread and brings it toward her face. She starts giggling as it approaches.

"So I just bang it into my face?" She's laughing louder now, drawing some amused looks from other tables.

"Not bang," I say. "Just, you know, make it face-adjacent." A bolt of inspiration strikes me. "Like an ice-cream cone! I've seen you eat one of those."

"Right. An ice-cream cone." Greta's holding the sandwich in front of her face now, and is eyeing it dubiously. "But that's soft. You don't really bite it."

She opens her mouth and leans forward, only to start laughing again. She sets the sandwich down for her fit of giggles.

Finally, with a deep breath, she hoists the sandwich, opens her mouth, and crams pastrami and rye between her teeth.

She giggles and chews, and she has pastrami on her cheek, but she's the cutest girl to ever fail to eat a sandwich like a normal person.

She's trying, though, just as I am heroically ignoring the glint of pointy forks at the table next to us.

All in all, it's a pretty great lunch.

AFTER LUNCH, we take a look at the gift shop before returning to the ship. Greta needs to prepare for her movie role the next day, and Pinky has a shift to work at the bar.

As we browse the mugs, t-shirts, and novelty oxygen masks, I pay close attention to see if Nana, Pinky, or Greta expresses particular interest in anything. Greta holds an oxygen mask up to her face to show it to me. It's gray, with big dark circles to see through and giant floppy ears attached to the top. The hose that attaches to the tank makes the entire thing look like an elephant.

She puts it down after we laugh, though, so I don't think she wants it.

The nice thing about living on a ship in space is that we don't need to own much, nor do we have space to store it. The down side of that is how hard it is to buy a present for someone in those circumstances. It can't be just any old thing, because it would take up what little space we have in our cabins, and it's always awkward to get rid of something you don't want when it was a gift. Especially if that person might visit your cabin and notice its absence.

We leave the gift shop empty-handed. I'm disappointed I

haven't solved my present-giving puzzle, but still hopeful I'll figure it out.

As we leave the station to return to the *Second Chance,* Nana is asking Greta and Pinky lots of questions about the movie they're going to be in. I fall behind to give them the chance to talk without creating a four-person blockade that would hinder anyone who might come from the opposite direction.

I notice an odd squeaking from the floor. Oh, that would be just my luck for the station to malfunction while I'm here. A loose floor tile, maybe, sending me plunging fifty feet below. Or a catastrophic structural failure, perhaps.

I hurry ahead. The odds of the culturally iconic International Space Station having a critical failure just as I walk over it are so infinitesimal that it's ridiculous to even consider. I'll have to work up those odds later, when I catch up on some of my other work, but I already know it's got to be at least five standard deviations away from a normal distribution.

But I'm still a redshirt, after all, and I hurry out of there, anyway.

2

As the holiday season progresses, Pinky has been gradually upping the cheer factor in her bar. It started with little robot snowmen. There were some up on the wall and smaller figures dotted the tables and the bar. I felt like this was a nod to me, and kind of a symbol of our shared interest in robot westerns. But then she added the light-up shoe display. After that, she hung a pair of giant dinosaur heads near the bar. They wore Santa hats, so I could only guess that she was blending Christmas with some other, more reptilian holiday.

Since I was last in, she's strung some multicolored lights and garlands with trumpets, gingerbread people, and, most inexplicably, wheels of cheese.

I can't keep up with all the different traditions from all the many planets, so I just do my best to roll with it.

Nothing thus far in the multi-celebration season has prepared me for the scene that awaits me at Pinky's bar. The post-dinner hour is in full swing, and the place is packed.

Everyone's shirtless.

Some wear Santa hats or headbands with little candy canes

mounted on tall stalks, but every single person is baring a lot more skin from the waist up than I'm accustomed to seeing outside of a shower room or the beach.

I approach the bar, feeling uncertain and oddly uncomfortable.

Why should I feel uncomfortable? I'm not the one showing my armpit hair to unwary passersby.

A Santa hat appears from below the bar, perched atop the head of someone standing upright. Pinky's face follows, then her bulging biceps, and then a sturdy-looking athletic bra. Finally, I get a view of a whole lot of pink washboard abs.

"Hey, Charlie. What can I get you?" She asks this as if nothing is out of the ordinary.

"Uh, just a ginger ale, I think. I have some work to do still." I try to keep my tone casual, as if I feel entirely normal about what's going on around me. "What's up with all the shirtlessness?"

"Oh, it's Tapp Zaff. It's where everyone goes shirtless and pretends they're at the beach. Kind of a celebration of the sun. Fun, right?"

"Oodles," I agree. "It's okay if I keep mine on, though, right?"

"Sure. Tapp Zaff is a totally do-your-own-thing kind of celebration."

"Great."

She hands me a glass but it isn't full of ginger ale.

"What's this?" I ask.

"Egg nog. You weren't really in the mood for ginger ale."

I take a cautious sip. It's delicious. Thick and creamy, with just a bit of cinnamon and nutmeg.

"You have a gift for choosing drinks for people," I tell her. "It's almost like a special power."

"Yeah, I do. It's too bad Greta's studying her lines," she says. "We could have had some fun tonight."

"Will you study your lines after work?"

"Nah. I've got them down already. Greta knows her lines too. She's just being fussy."

I love Pinky's self-confidence. I wish I had just a tiny bit of that. "Are you excited about being in a movie?"

She shrugs. "It'll be interesting. Something different. We'll see."

She doesn't seem excited, but she's cool that way.

I decide to get her advice on my gift situation. "Do you have any ideas of what I can get for Greta? I want to get her something she'll really like."

Pinky points at me. "You're lucky. Some girls dream of expensive jewelry or designer hats. Greta's much more practical."

"I'm glad for that," I agree. "But it does make gift giving difficult. I mean, with her luck, if she really wanted something, it would somehow appear."

"True." Pinky plucks a red and white striped straw and chews on the end thoughtfully. "You should think of something unique. Something that can't be bought in a store."

"You mean, I should knit her a sweater or something?"

Pinky asks with the straw between her teeth, "Do you know how to knit?"

"No."

"Then not that. Keep thinking."

"Okay." I finish off my egg nog. "I should go. Those statistics aren't going to analyze themselves."

Pinky points the mangled end of the straw at me. "Have fun, then. I'll see you tomorrow."

"Sure. Enjoy your Tapp Zaff."

"I will," she says, grabbing a huge mug and filling it with beer. "I get fantastic tips whenever I flex my muscles."

Pinky likes to tease me sometimes, but I have no doubt that she's telling the truth about this one.

THE NEXT MORNING, I'm pleased to find that no one is attempting to assimilate me while I sleep. My hope is that Nana heeded my request to stop breaking in, but I took the extra precaution yesterday of asking Gus, the head porter, to upgrade the lock on my cabin door. Just to be sure.

I go down the hall to shower. As I get ready for the day, I feel a sense of optimism stealing over me.

Such a sense, I assure you, is previously unknown to my people. But I feel good, knowing Greta is going to have fun with her movie, and that somehow, some way, I'm going to find the right gifts for her, Pinky, and even Nana.

I don't know how I'm going to manage it, but I will.

Gus strides my way just as I'm returning to my cabin. "Hey, Gus. Thanks again for getting my lock upgraded. It did the trick."

"I'm glad, Mr. Kenny. When our guests are happy, I'm happy."

I've never known someone so dedicated to his job. Gus refuses to use my first name, and usually talks like a commercial. Lots of platitudes and assurances.

The elevator has been giving him fits in recent weeks, and it's secretly been fun to watch him quietly freak out about it.

I feel a little guilty about that, but I can't help it. The guy is just so tightly wound.

Something wicked within me prompts me to ask, "Any luck with the *Chance 3000?*"

His carefully schooled professional demeanor cracks into a grimace. "We've had no further reports of the lightstream malfunctioning, and I thought we'd returned the elevator to factory settings. It seemed to behave normally for three days. But then a family with young children told me that it had spent a good ten minutes regaling them with dirty limericks."

He sighs, and seems to be aging before my very eyes.

I take pity on him. I can't rat out my friend, but I can give him some hints. "Around the time that the *Chance 3000* announced itself, had anything unusual happened? Any strange people come aboard? Or...could someone vengeful have been offended?"

I'm in a delicate position. I know he already suspects Pinky, and I know Pinky is responsible. But she's my friend, so I'm trying to be subtle.

Gus shakes his head, then freezes. His eyes widen and bore straight into me. "Are you telling me—"

I hold my hands in front of myself defensively. "I don't know anything for sure. But is it possible that something you said could have been overheard and taken personally? By someone who has a low tolerance for insults and a large capacity for retribution?"

Gus pales. His worst nightmare has been confirmed. "If that were the case, how would I mend the situation?"

"I'm not sure," I say. "I don't think a simple apology would be enough. There'd have to be a certain...what's the word...penance?"

I see worry and frustration on his face. All of a sudden, his shoulders slump, his professionalism falls away, and he utters a curse word so foul that I'm not even going to share it with you.

Because I care about you and your ability to sleep at night.

But never mind that. Gus is undergoing a transformation before my very eyes. Something's happening. I truly meant to help, but I seem to have touched the last nerve holding Gus together.

He unbuttons his perfectly starched and pressed uniform jacket. "I think I'm going to retire."

"Right now?" A minute ago, he was going about like normal and now he's giving up. What have I done? Damn my luck!

I should have pretended I didn't know anything about Pinky and the *Chance 3000*.

Greta's location on board the space station must be too far

from the ship. Or maybe it's that she's been out of proximity for too long. I'm not sure exactly how my bad luck and her good luck battle it out and settle on something somewhere in the middle, but I'm pretty sure something has reached a tipping point in a bad way.

Gus looks philosophical. Resigned. I imagine this is what a man looks like when he's marching off to war, knowing he'll never return. "First, I'll apologize. I'll even let her poke me in the forehead in that really demeaning way she likes. And then I'm taking the day off to think over what I'm going to do with my life," Gus announced. "If you need anything, you can contact my assistant, Fabrizio. Please enjoy your stay aboard the *Second Chance*."

Okay, now I know he's cracked a little. He's just delivered his standard line, which he hasn't said to me since I started living aboard the ship. It's like he's reverted to his own factory settings. Except for the whole reevaluating-his-life thing. That bit is new.

For a moment, I'm frozen with uncertainty. My bad luck is like a plague that, gone unchecked, could take down the entire starship.

Then I come to my senses. I need to get to Greta. Getting back into her sphere of influence is the only way to stem the tsunami of badness that is surely coming my way.

I throw my toiletry bag into my cabin and bolt for the exit.

Just like that, I'm no longer Charlie Kenny, adventurer. I'm once again Charlie Kenny, redshirt. My chest is tight with anxiety, and I feel like there's not enough air on the ship.

Still, I don't sprint. I carefully hurry. I know darn well that running will result in a catastrophic fall, perhaps out of an airlock with an inconveniently timed malfunction.

At least I have experience on my side.

As I'm fleeing, I expect something ridiculous to happen. Something nearly impossible. Something that could only happen to me.

Nothing crazy occurs.

However, I do nearly run into Nana as she steps out of her cabin.

"Charlie! What's going on?" Nana asks, falling into step with me. She's been around for decades longer than I have, and knows that if someone's running from something, you don't even stop to think about it. You start running, too.

Now we're both carefully trotting through the ship toward the space dock.

"*Kenogu*," I say. I'm out of breath, and it's a Mebdarian word anyway, so I doubt she'll understand.

But being a cyborg comes with certain unexpected areas of knowledge, and she says, "Ah, I see. What do we do about it?"

Pinky taught me about the concept of kenogu, which basically means that shit happens and it's up to you to make the best of it. Or, at the least, to survive it.

It's a darn good word, really.

"Greta." I can only get one word out because between the anxiety and the jogging, I don't have breath to spare.

"Gotcha. I'm on it!"

Nana runs ahead of me, somehow grabs me, and flings me onto her back.

Now I'm getting a piggyback ride from my nana, and we are *hauling*. I can barely make out the startled expressions of the people who see us bolting by like the most unlikely competitors at a corporate picnic ever.

We make it onto the station and Nana busts right through the security checkpoint for the production crew. Between her speed and stealth and our element of surprise, we blow right through there.

A sign ahead points the way to the dressing rooms.

"That way!" I stab a finger to the left.

"On it!" Nana shouts.

We start down a hallway and there are like a dozen doors. Rather than take time to stop and knock, Nana gives each one a gentle kick as we go by. Instead of kicking the doors in, she merely makes a small dent.

Naturally the ruckus makes all of the doors open, and startled people emerge.

And there she is. Sweet Greta with her great kindness and understanding, her sense of adventure and even greater sense of humor.

She stands in the hallway, where Nana and I have stopped. For whatever reason, I remain on her back.

The love of my life stares at us, her eyes wide. "What the hell?"

"Kenogu," I say simply.

"Oh, shit." Greta immediately goes into damage control mode. "Everyone, back in your dressing rooms! Don't come out until I say so!"

She gestures toward her room. "Hurry."

Nana pauses, though, on the way in, noticing that no one has done as Greta said. "Well you heard her! Get your asses in there before I give them a pounding you won't soon forget!"

Greta closes her dressing room door behind us. Nana deposits me on a padded bench, and I put my head in my hands, lamenting the ruins of the day.

This was supposed to be a great day for Greta, and I've gone and screwed it up. Her dressing room is little, but has an expensive-looking dressing table and a pile of luxury snack foods on a side table. She should have been able to enjoy this experience.

"What happened?" she asks, eyes intense and voice urgent.

"We messed up the formula somehow," I said. "I was too far from you, or outside of your zone of influence too long, or something." I take a breath. "I broke Gus."

Greta gasps. "Oh no. What happened?"

"We were talking, and I asked about the elevator, and suddenly he was regretting his whole life, I think. He said he was going to reconsider his choices, and maybe retire. And he quit working in the middle of a shift."

Greta puts a hand to her mouth. "Wow. Okay, not as bad as I feared. I thought, like, you physically broke him. I mean, this is bad, too, but we can fix it."

Now that I'm with her, the tightness in my chest is loosening. My panic is fading. Nothing horrific has ever happened to Greta. Since meeting me, she's seen highly improbable things, and somewhat inconveniencing things, but nothing awful. As long as I don't stray too far, we'll all be fine.

"This came on kind of fast. I've only been over here a couple hours. Are you carrying your luck stone?" Greta asks, frowning.

In my head, I envision the little green rock she gave me, saying that she'd held it for a while and it might have absorbed a little of her luck. "No. I left it in my cabin while I showered, so I wouldn't lose it."

"Maybe that's why." She looks thoughtful.

Nana's standing by the door like a soldier expecting an invasion force.

It's kind of comforting, actually.

"Okay, here's what we're going to do," Greta announces. "I still have a few scenes to do before I can leave, but you two will stay with me. It may get a little boring for you, but I already got permission for you to visit the set. Pinky doesn't have any scenes until tomorrow, but I'm going to see if she'll come, anyway. I'd just feel better if she were keeping an eye out for you. I'll have her grab your luck stone, too."

"Are you sure?" I ask. "I don't want to mess up anything for you."

"Mess up the movie?" She shakes her head. "It'll be fine. Don't worry."

"Someone's coming!" Nana looks ready to annihilate whoever it is.

"Hang on!" Greta hops across the room and wedges herself between Nana and the side of the door that opens. She peeks out.

A smooth, male voice exclaims,"Darling! What's happening here? I heard there was a commotion."

Greta straightens and opens the door the rest of the way. I see a stylish human in a button-up shirt and a pair of slacks.

"It's all under control now, Alex. The show will go on!"

"That's what I like to hear." Alex edged into the room. "Who are these guests of yours that have gotten my people all worked up?"

He's good-looking, rich, and probably famous.

"Rose, Charlie, this is my director, Alex. Alex, these are the friends I was telling you about."

He dismisses me after the briefest look, but Nana's got his attention. "A cyborg?"

"Yes, she'll be no trouble, I promise." Greta smiles reassuringly.

"Trouble?" Alex looks offended. "Are you kidding? This is fantastic! We could put her in the temple scene. The audience will love it."

"Me, in a movie?" Nana looks enchanted with the idea.

"You're made for it!" Alex insists. "This is going to be my biggest film yet."

He looks thrilled, Greta appears excited, and Nana is clearly beside herself.

The only one not enthusiastic about the day's events is me.

I DON'T WANT to hurt Greta's feelings, but watching a movie being filmed is as much fun as watching metal rust. It takes about as long, too.

Nana is intrigued with the process, though, and Pinky, who has joined us, seems relatively entertained.

The cast and crew recovered almost immediately from the scene that Nana and I made, and now they're filming a deeply serious scene with Greta. Her character is gravely ill, and looking for perspective in her life.

"I wish life came with a guarantee," Greta says for the five billionth time, but still managing to sound distraught. "If I just knew whether I had a month, or three, or a year, I'd know what to do next."

"Cut!" Alex sweeps in. "Perfect. Let's swap out the set for the next scene. Everyone take a fifteen-minute break."

A small army of people either bolt from the set or dash onto it, rumpling up the bed and whisking away the teacups used in the current scene.

"Do you guys want to see the green room?" Greta asks. "They usually have some good food set out."

Pinky's already on her feet. "Free food? Oh yeah."

In the green room, which is actually a comfortingly dull beige color, I snack on some fresh vegetables and a bit of creamy dip. Greta and Nana eat nothing, while Pinky seems to have made it her mission to make sure that no poor production assistant has to put away any leftovers.

In spite of the relapse of bad luck earlier, I'm feeling only mildly on edge. As I fill a cup with water and take a sip, I hear a faint chittering noise, like the one I heard the day before in an entirely different part of the station.

I tilt my head to the side, listening, but the sound has gone.

"What's wrong?" Nana asks.

"Nothing," I say. "I heard kind of a squeak or something."

"I heard it too." She tapped her cybernetically enhanced ear. "I've heard it on and off the whole time I've been here. Think something's wrong?"

"Some places are just creaky," I say. "I'm sure it's fine."

"If you say so." Nana sounds doubtful. "I've never been off Earth, so I guess this is what a space station could sound like."

It occurs to me that this is a big moment for our family. Two Kennys have left Earth to travel the stars, and outside of possibly destroying Gus' sense of self and his will to live, nothing major has happened.

Greta comes over and puts her hand on my arm. "We should get back."

"Sure. You were great in that last scene, by the way."

She beams at me as we head back to the set. "Thanks! The next scene is more upbeat, when my character has recovered. I think it'll be easier. The serious stuff is hard."

"I'm sure you'll be terrific. You're—" A sudden crushing pain just above my elbow makes me freeze.

It's Pinky's hand. She's staring at the set.

I follow her gaze toward a tall cage. As we watch a production assistant fussing with it, I hear a chittering sound.

"Blagrooks." Pinky announces it like she's pronouncing the end of the world. "They've brought in real blagrooks."

I've never seen one of the creatures in person. As we get closer, I see they're just as I've seen in pictures. They have long snouts and tall, pointed ears. Their eyes are tiny, beady, and show no hint of intelligence whatsoever. I feel I'm staring into the face of a remorseless, hateful stupidity unlike anything I've ever witnessed.

I can see why Pinky doesn't like them.

Fortunately, she's released my arm. I rub it surreptitiously, while her eyes are on the blagrooks. "That's what I heard earlier," I say. "That sound they make. I heard it yesterday, too."

"Since when are there live blagrooks in this movie?" Pinky demands, stomping off toward Alex.

Greta and I hurry after her. Nana remains to watch the creatures.

"What idiot brings blagrooks aboard a space station?" Pinky demands.

Alex blinks, but recovers quickly. "Don't worry. They have two trained handlers with them at all times. They won't harm anything. The producer decided to use live blagrooks instead of props, for realism."

"And the station approved?" Pinky glares.

"Not at first," Alex admitted. "They had a lot of transportation and handling requirements, and we had to pay for a special insurance rider. But we got it worked out."

"Count me out of your movie, then," Pinky says. "I don't work with blagrooks, or people foolish enough to play games with them."

Greta looks stricken. "Oh, Pinky, are you sure?"

"As sure as I'm pink. You stay if you want, but I'm out of here." Pinky turns on her heel and stalks out.

Greta throws a pleading look to Alex. "Give me a minute to talk to her, okay?"

Alex frowns. "I don't know. If she has an attitude like that, she doesn't belong on my set. But...I don't have anyone else lined up for her role." He sighs. "Okay, give it a try, but hurry back. We're on the clock."

Greta runs after Pinky, and I follow at a slower pace. I don't know what Greta's planning to say, or why Pinky's so mad, but there's no point in me hanging around the set. Nana remains behind, watching the blagrooks.

I don't know if she's fascinated or horrified. Either way, at least she has an eye on them.

By the time I catch up to my friends in the hall, they're already talking.

"Are you sure you want to go, Pinky? It's okay if you do, but I don't want you to regret your decision. You were looking forward to being in a movie."

"Nah. I liked the green room food, and seeing myself on the

screen would have been fun, but I can't support something that involves the use of real blagrooks. I have principles."

Greta nods. "Okay, as long as you're sure. Is it okay with you if I go ahead and do the movie? It's just today and tomorrow, and I've done a lot of preparing..." she trails off, looking sheepish.

"You gotta make your own choice. I get it." Pinky holds up a fist and Greta bumps it with her own. "Keep an eye out, Charlie. If anything looks strange, get our girl out of here."

"I'll do my best." I refrain from adding that this doesn't ensure much, because we all already know this. More importantly, Greta has her luck, which is far more valuable than my feeble attempts to guard her.

"Good man." Pinky claps me gently on the shoulder. "I'll catch you two later, then."

"That's too bad," Greta sighs as we slowly make our way back to the set. "I wish things had worked out differently."

When we arrive, Nana crooks her finger at me. I join her while Greta explains the situation to Alex.

"I've been listening to these things and measuring their acoustic output," Nana says without preamble. "There is absolutely no way we could have heard them from the green room."

I have a familiar sinking feeling. "Are you sure?"

"Completely. Some of those things have escaped and are loose on the station."

I'm nervous as I watch Greta act out the scene. She was right. This scenario is much more upbeat, and the work is going faster. I've sent Nana to investigate with her clever cyborg hearing to try to figure out what we can do about the blagrook escapees. I figure if anyone's going to get to the bottom of that situation, it's got to be her.

Once we have some facts to relay, we'll go right to the station administration office when Greta's scene is done. Then they can deal with the issue.

I hope the film doesn't get shut down. I don't want her to be disappointed.

When the filming for the day wraps up, everyone claps and the set becomes a hive of activity. The blagrook handlers are wheeling the giant cage away while other production assistants have begun tearing down the set to prepare for the next day's work.

"You were great," I tell Greta as we head back to her dressing room. "I really believed you were happy that your scientist boyfriend had discovered a cure for your disease."

"Yeah?" She's shiny with glee.

"Completely."

"Thanks, Charlie. I just have a little more to do in a scene tomorrow, then I'm done. Other than the part about Pinky, this has been fun."

"Any idea what they're going to do to fill her role?" I ask.

"Alex is planning to do it. He used to act before he started directing, so it'll be fine."

I nod. "Want to have dinner at Pinky's? They're doing a Tapp Zaff celebration today."

"I love Tapp Zaff! It's more fun in a sunny place, of course, but people usually start playing silly games and dancing."

"Great. Do you want me to wait outside your dressing room while you—"

A crashing riot of noise and screaming interrupts me.

Oh.

Crap.

Greta's eyes meet mine, sober with understanding. "Blagrooks?"

"It's the only reasonable explanation."

"What do you think happened?"

"Nothing good, but we're going in there, aren't we?" I know

Greta. There's no way she's leaving when somebody might need help.

"Yeah." She grabs my hand for reassurance.

Not for hers. For my reassurance.

Here we go.

3

THE MOVIE SET looks more like a post-apocalyptic nightmare than an uplifting drama. The blagrook cage is on its side, dented and obviously now devoid of any blagrooks.

A production assistant is wrapping Alex's arm while another dabs at a bloody slash on his forehead.

"What happened?" Greta asks.

"A boom mic fell, tipped over the cage, and caused a piece of lighting to fall." Alex looks dazed.

"It fell on you?" I ask.

"No. I tried to grab a blagrook to keep it from escaping. I shouldn't have done that."

I pull aside the assistant who'd wrapped his arm. "Blagrook scratches can be toxic. You need to get Alex to the medbay."

"He said he didn't want to leave the crew." The man's forehead creases with indecision.

"Doesn't matter what he wants. He could get really sick if he doesn't go right away." I know this because sometimes when I can't sleep, I stay up searching for disaster scenarios and what to do.

This is the first time that's actually come in handy.

A scrabbling sound behind us makes me whip around, but not fast enough. A blagrook has crawled out from behind something and launched itself at us.

No way I'm going to let its talons touch Greta. I step in front of her to put myself between her and the monster.

A dark blur rushes in front of me, and suddenly the blagrook is flying away from us. It hits a wall and falls to the ground, still.

"Pinky!"

I wish I could say it was Greta who yelled that while I stoically stood alongside, having just sacrificed myself for the woman I love. But no. That high-pitched squeal was me.

Sigh.

I *almost* did something cool.

On the bright side, Pinky stands before us, holding some sort of bat with nails or something sticking through it. Maybe it's a primitive cudgel. Or a mace. Which one has the spiky bits on it? Weapons aren't my forte.

Fortunately, they're Pinky's specialty and she's clearly ready for a fight.

"I had a bad feeling, so I went for my blagrook bat and came back. Good thing too. That thing was about to eat Charlie's face."

I roll my eyes at the hyperbole, determined to believe that she is indeed speaking hyperbole.

"Where's Nana Rose?" Pinky asks. "I'm going to need her help cleaning up this mess."

"She's scouting the station. She can hear the things."

"Good." Pinky nods. "We have to be sure to get them all. If you leave even one, you'll be re-infested in no time."

"There were six in the cage," Greta says. "Minus that one."

We look to the one Pinky smashed.

"There are more than that," I say. "Nana and I both heard them before the ones in the cage broke out."

"Oh, no." Greta looks to Pinky. "How do we get rid of them?"

Pinky swings her bat up to rest on her shoulder. "We go hunting."

IN THIS GAME OF WHACK-A-BLAGROOK, I'm pretty much superfluous. Greta and I creep along behind Nana, who stalks the station with her head tilted, listening. Every now and then she yells, "Get it, Pinky!"

That's when Pinky, with destruction and pure joy in her eyes, steps in and smashes the hell out of whatever Nana's pointing at. A wall. A chair. An electrical panel. That last one got exciting there for a minute, when there were sparks and popping sounds and the smell of singed blagrook hair.

It's not a good smell.

We comb the entire station, even areas that are usually off-limits. Then we double back and whack a few more blagrooks. The amount of time between Pinky's violent outbursts gradually lengthens, until it's been two full hours since we last found one.

"We might have gotten them all." Nana has her ear pressed to the door of an elevator shaft. "I'm not hearing any more."

"I guess that's good." Pinky examines the end of her bat.

"Definitely good," I say. "Any more holes in this place and they might decide to scuttle it and build a new one."

I'm joking, of course. So far, Pinky has masterfully avoided creating a hull breach or damaging any critical systems.

"I think I'll go check on Alex," Greta says. "Make sure he's okay, and see if there's anything I need to do before I go back to the *Second Chance.*"

"I'll go with you." I'm no help to Pinky and Nana in this matter, and I'd seen enough dead blagrook to last me a lifetime.

As we make our way back to the movie set, I ask, "Think they'll still film tomorrow?"

"If they can, they will. It's too expensive to delay if they can avoid it. But if Alex can't work, there's no other choice."

I keep my opinion of Alex to myself, which means I have a whole lot of silent judging going on. It seems fair that he was the one to get hurt, since he was the idiot who brought the blagrooks on board.

Carefully, I say, "I hope this doesn't affect your appearance in the movie."

She shrugs as we approach the set. "If there's a delay, it's just too bad. The *Second Chance* takes off for Alpha Centauri in two days."

"They'd probably wait if you asked," I say. Truth be told, if Greta truly wanted to remain on the station, I'm certain that something would happen to make it possible.

"I'd never ask for the ship to delay because of me. That's my job. This movie thing is just for fun. It's not a big deal if it doesn't work out."

She waves to a production assistant as we come down the hallway of dressing rooms. "Hey, Albie. Do you know where Alex is?"

"Yeah, he's in the cutting room, looking at the dailies. Go on in, maybe you can see a rough cut of one of your scenes."

"He must not have been as hurt as he looked," I say.

Albie shakes his head. "He had some pretty nasty cuts. But Alex is obsessed with his work. That's why he's so successful."

Greta leads me away from the dressing rooms and down an intersecting corridor.

"I wonder what these rooms are usually used for," I say.

"Public relations stuff. Places to put reporters, film crews, visiting dignitaries, that sort of thing." She opens the door to a darkened room.

On a large screen, I see my recent past replaying itself. I watch the boom mic fall into the blagrook cage, just as Alex had described it to me. The cage topples, gets damaged, and the creatures start squeezing out through the opened space.

The angle shifts and I see Alex rushing forward, grabbing at a blagrook, and then the thing viciously attacks him.

The film abruptly jumps and I'm surprised to see myself appear, along with Greta. A blagrook launches itself at us and suddenly Pinky's there, taking aim and knocking it across the room.

The angle shifts and there's Pinky, larger than life, looking cooler and more composed than any movie hero I've ever seen.

She swings her bat up to rest on her shoulder and says, "We go hunting."

"Perfect!" Alex exclaims. "Now switch to the surveillance cameras."

I see a series of clips showing Nana leading the way around the station, and Pinky pounding blagrook after blagrook.

"Alex?" Greta finally asks. "Are you okay?"

He turns, surprised to see us. "Greta, darling! I'm more than okay. I'm a genius!"

Considering I just watched him try to grab a blagrook with his bare hands, I strongly disagree with his assessment. I keep my mouth closed, though.

"What do you mean?" Greta asks. From the careful way she says it, I know she's thinking the exact same thing.

"I'm shifting the focus of the story. I'm going with an alien invasion theme." Alex is radiating excitement.

"But it's titled 'Her Husband's Secret.'" Greta looks bewildered. "It's a psychological drama. There are no aliens."

"There are now," he says. "I'm changing the title to 'Attack of the Blagrooks.' It's going to be an action thriller."

Words have failed Greta. She's staring at Alex like he's the alien.

He takes no notice, looking right past us. Amazingly, he

becomes even more animated. I feel like he's going to hurt himself if he doesn't calm down.

I glance over my shoulder to see Pinky and Nana coming in behind us.

"And there are my stars!" Alex exclaims.

THE DAY after the blagrook escape, Alex has us all back on the set. The place now looks like an industrial waste dump.

Pinky is much happier with her role now. Instead of being a sage, she's now a take-no-crap customs official. Most importantly, she gets to smash stuff.

We spend the morning watching her happily smashing stuff, and truly, I've never seen Pinky happier. Nana smashes a few things too, and even Greta has a scene where she fires a pistol which, we're told, will result in a huge explosion once they create the effects.

Even I'm placed in a few scenes, since I show up on the surveillance cameras and it would be strange not to have me appear anywhere else. I only have a few lines, consisting mainly of things like, "Oh no!" and, "Look out!"

Mostly, it's just my job to look nervous or scared. Fortunately, that is my wheelhouse, and I feel like I'm able to deliver a wildly believable performance.

Pinky, as the star of the show, has more to do than the rest of us. She likes the talking part a lot less than the smashing part, though. Pinky will repeat the same line four times. Ask her for a fifth time and she gets pissy.

Alex is learning to conserve his efforts in having her deliver lines.

"Okay," he calls. "That was great. Now, let's do the line 'Let's go hunting' again, with you walking off camera."

"No." Pinky doesn't move.

Alex is used to people jumping at his command. Working with Pinky is nothing like that.

"What?" He blinks in confusion.

"We did that," Pinky says. "I've said 'let's go hunting' about a hundred times, and I've done tons of walking. And I was great. So you work with what you already have on that camera of yours. Are we done here?"

Alex's bewilderment makes me want to laugh. Later, I will. For now, I clamp my lips together.

He uncertainly asks, "Can we get you stepping forward and doing a thumbs-up?"

"I like it. Let's do that." Pinky sets her bat aside. After sticking her thumbs up several times, she says. "Oh, I know. How about some dancing? Like, maybe I've blasted all the blagrooks, and decide to celebrate by having a dance party?"

Alex's face glazes over, like he's partially phase-shifting into another dimension but part of him remains here, too. He realizes now what he's done in eliciting Pinky's help, and regardless of what happens with this movie, I'm certain that this is a lesson that will affect him for the rest of his life, in some sort of way.

"Uh...okay. Yeah..."

And there it is. I'm pretty sure I've just watched a man lose his will to live.

Pinky sometimes has that effect on people.

Things finish up pretty fast after that. Pinky impresses the crew with her legitimately sick dance moves—that's sick as in really great, not as in ill or gross or something—then we're free to go. Our job here is done.

Alex half-heartedly invites us to a wrap party, but Pinky shuts him down cold.

"No way," she tells him. "I have enough to do for the holidays. You take care of your own damn gifts and ribbons and stuff."

Greta whispers in my ear, "Should we tell her what a wrap party really is?"

I shake my head. "Not after a line like that."

So we return to the *Second Chance*. We've ruined a movie, starred in a different movie, and saved a station from a blagrook attack. Plus, Pinky got to smash a lot of stuff.

All in all, it's been a good couple of days.

I SPEND the rest of that afternoon and evening catching up on some work. When I send it in to my employers, I wonder if any of them will see the movie. Wouldn't that be something?

I'm glad to be back to the regular routine, though. The brush with my redshirt luck has left me unharmed, but craving the comfort of predictability.

Greta meets me for dinner at Pinky's, and when I get there, the décor has changed. The garlands are gone, and giant candy canes have appeared in their place. They hang on the walls, dangle from the ceilings, and Pinky even has one behind the bar, propped up to one side.

"Need some help mixing drinks tonight?" I ask, raising my voice to be heard. "The place is packed!"

"Maybe later," Pinky says. "Tonight is Martian Christmas, so everyone's having the traditional egg nog and pecan sandies. It's easy to keep up with."

She puts a glass of egg nog in front of each of us, then adds a basket of little round cookies. "Is Nana Rose coming?"

I bite into a cookie and it's delicious. "No, she said she was tired."

"I didn't know cyborgs get tired," Greta says.

"Neither did I. Usually Nana has more energy than I do. But cyborg or not, she's still elderly." I want another cookie, but I should have a meal first. "What's the traditional Martian dinner, anyway?"

"Beef stroganoff ration packets," Pinky answers.

"Seriously? Why?"

She shrugs. "Their colonization was rough, I guess, and sometimes things stick. Who cares? Some traditions suck and should be ignored."

"I guess so. Would tomato soup and a grilled cheese sandwich be appropriate?"

"That sounds good," Greta says. "Two orders of that, please, Pinky."

While Pinky sends our order to the kitchen, I decide to segue into the mistletoe thing. All this talk of tradition seems like the perfect time.

"What does your family do for the holiday?" I ask.

"Oh, the usual." She smiles fondly. "We celebrate Rotation Day. It's kind of an acknowledgment of the year, you know, going around the sun another time. We fly kites, eat pretzels, and insult each other. It's nice."

Did I hear that right? "Insult each other?"

"Just jokingly. We tease one another about all the things we didn't do during the year, or unfortunate things we did do. It's not mean. It's meant to be motivational for the year ahead." She toys with the cookie basket, scooting it around in a circle.

"You miss home, don't you?" I never realized it, because she rarely mentions her home or family. Probably because talking about it makes her homesick.

"Sure. Doesn't everyone miss home during the holidays?" She smiles.

"I don't. I'd much rather be here." I remember my intention of laying the mistletoe groundwork. "Although...I do miss the mistletoe tradition."

"I don't think I know that one. What is it?"

I chuckle. "Well, it's kind of silly, but fun. For some reason, people a long time ago used to hang up this tree fungus called mistletoe. When two people happened to find themselves standing under it, they kissed."

Her forehead crinkles. "Tree fungus?"

"Yeah. I don't know why. Traditions are strange sometimes. But people always laughed and had fun."

"Did you kiss a lot of girls under the mistletoe?" She grins at me.

"No. I was never lucky enough to end up standing under it with anyone I wanted to kiss, and since I didn't want to kiss my Uncle Cecil, I made sure to keep my distance."

She giggles. "So there's an element of risk involved with this game, too."

I'd never thought of it that way. "Yeah. Strategy too, I guess. Trying to avoid the kisses you don't want, and get the ones you do."

"It sounds fun." She sips her egg nog. "Earth holidays feature this drink too, right? It's yummy."

"Yup. The other planets in my solar system did a lot of borrowing of Earth traditions, so we share a lot of similarities." I frown, then add, "Except for Mercury. Those people are kind of crazy."

Our food arrives and we enjoy the evening. It's a little boisterous at times, with some impromptu singing of carols and occasional throwing of streamers, but it's still a nice, low-key way to end the day.

Afterward, when I get back to my cabin, I try again to contact Gus. I've been assured that he's fine and has returned to his work as usual, but I think he's avoiding me. I don't know if he's embarrassed or if he's one french fry short of a basket. For the well-being of the ship and crew, I need to check into that.

Tomorrow. After the last couple of days, I'm in need of a good, long sleep.

Before tackling the Gus situation, I need to handle the Pinky situation. I've asked her to my cabin for a serious talk.

My room always looks small, but with her inside, it's positively miniscule. We bravely ignore this situation, though, in order to focus on the issue at hand.

"Pinky," I begin. "Gus is about to have a mental breakdown. He may have already had a small one."

She gazes at me impassively. "What's that got to do with me?"

This is tricky. I need to be careful how I present this. "As much fun as the *Chance 3000* has been, Gus has gotten a lot of customer complaints about it."

To preserve Pinky's feelings, I'm characterizing being terrorized by an elevator as "fun."

She stares at me.

"You meant for that to happen, right?" I prod.

"Yeah, you got me. If you ask me, the ship's much better this way, too. Much more fun."

"Oh yeah, for sure," I agree. I don't mention all the times it most certainly was not fun, but the *Chance 3000* has had a decent moment here or there. "But you know how much Gus prides himself on doing a good job. He's starting to crack, and if something doesn't change, we're going to need a new head porter."

I hold my breath, hoping I've managed to say all the right things in just the right way.

Pinky frowns. "I didn't like how he disrespected me. There's a price for that. But I didn't mean to make him go completely batshit. I don't want to have to break in a new head porter, either."

"Do you think you could uninstall the *Chance 3000*?"

"But things would get so boring." She rubs her chin. "How about if it only activates when there are no guests in the elevator? That way, the guests don't complain, Gus doesn't crack his nut, and the rest of us still get to enjoy the refreshing change of pace?"

I'm guessing "crack his nut" is a Mebdarian euphemism for

going crazy. Sometimes out here in space, a person just has to lean into context.

For my own part, I have not found all of the *Chance 3000*'s antics refreshing, but this might be the best deal I can wrangle.

"Let's give it a try," I suggest. "How long would it take you to make the change?"

She studies the fingernail of her right index finger. "Eh. Twenty minutes, probably."

"Great. If you go ahead and do that now, Gus could begin his day with the lovely surprise of a sudden stop to the elevator complaints."

Pinky picks at the nail. "I want him to apologize."

Uh oh. "What?"

"He insulted me, and my profession. He acted like being a bartender was beneath the job of head porter. It isn't, and I want him to say so."

"Everyone here knows how vital you are to the ship." I'm not just flattering her. Pinky's bar is wildly popular, and the reason Greta decided to live on this particular ship. "I'm sure he didn't mean it the way it sounded."

"Fine. If he apologizes, and means it, I'll do it."

"How will you know if he means it?" I ask.

"Oh, I'll know."

I'm not so sure about that. That was how we got into this problem in the first place.

But all I can do is smile bravely. "Okay, then! I'll talk to Gus, we'll get things ironed out, and we'll all be one big happy family, just in time for the holidays."

Pinky shoots me a suspicious look, like I'm trying to pull one over on her.

"I mean it," I say. "I wouldn't want to be anywhere else, and I want everyone here to be happy."

Her expression softens. "Okay, Charlie. You win. As a gesture of goodwill, and because I'm still in a good mood about becoming a movie star, I'll go right now and fix the elevator. But if Gus doesn't live up to his end of the bargain, I can change it right back."

"He will. Of course he will. How could he not, when you're such a peach?"

Pinky brightens. "You bet I am. Do you want to help me put up some decorations later?"

"More holiday decorations in the bar? Could they possibly fit?"

"Not the bar. The corridors. They're dull. I think the guests will appreciate a more festive atmosphere. A lot of them are traveling to spend time with their families."

"True," I agree. "And the ones who are traveling for work or whatever could certainly use a little extra cheer."

"Yeah! Let's do it!" Pinky stands and slaps her hands together.

"Okay!" I stand, too. "Right after the elevator thing."

She points at me.

She has a very imposing point.

"I see what you did there. But it's fine. Let's make the *Second Chance* the happiest place in the galaxy."

"Ha ha ha!" Pinky exclaims as she hangs a wreath opposite the shower room.

"That's ho ho ho, actually." I'm sticking some feathered pom poms to the wall. I don't know what holiday they're for, but they're kind of cute.

"Ho? Why?" She slaps some blue stars into my hands.

"Nobody knows why. It just is."

"Oh. Okay. Ho ho ho, then!" She gestures at me to start sticking the stars to the wall.

"Are these pentagrams or stars of David?" I flip through them, but they're all ambiguous.

"Don't you know?" She stands next to me and studies them.

"No. Either would make sense for a holiday thing, but the two belong to very different groups."

Pinky shrugs. "I guess they can be multipurpose."

I shrug, too, because that actually makes sense to me. We can't possibly cover every single holiday in existence, but we're doing our best to bring something of significance for all the people traveling on the ship during the holiday season.

She begins singing a song about a lecherous ocelot that has me scanning the corridor to make sure no guests are coming.

"What holiday is that one from, Pinky?"

She adjusts a bit of tinsel so that it hangs just so. "Oh, it's not a holiday song. It's a new release from Revnar VIII. Catchy chorus, don't you think?"

"Yeah, you bet."

"You think Nana Rose will come help?" Pinky asks. "I haven't seen much of her since the blagrook incident."

"I think it tired her out," I say. "I'm a little concerned about her, actually. I'll check in on her when we're done with this."

She tugs the last couple of stars out of my hands. "Go ahead and do it now. I'll feel better knowing she's okay, and you will, too."

Deep down, Pinky's a big softy.

Deep *deep* down. Like in those movies where there's seemingly no floor, and someone drops a coin and waits to hear it hit bottom and it never does. That kind of deep down.

"Okay. I'll catch up to you later, then."

She gives me a one-handed thumbs-up and returns to her festive efforts.

AT NANA'S CABIN, I cautiously tap on the door. She's proven her hearing is excellent, and startling her seems like a bad idea.

She doesn't answer, so after I stand there like a dingus staring at her door for two solid minutes, I tap again.

The door opens, and Nana joins me in the hall, closing the door behind her. But not before I saw what was going on in her room.

"Nana," I say. "Have you organized an underground canasta game?"

"No." Her voice has gone up in that way that tells me she's lying.

"Nana."

She sighs. "So what? We're all adults."

"You know that organized gambling is prohibited on interstellar ships. Jurisdiction gets super tricky on that kind of thing, so it's just banned. You couldn't wait until we got to Alpha Centauri to play some canasta?"

Nana sighs and leans back against the cabin door. "Look, Charlie, I didn't want to hurt your feelings. I really like seeing you more often, and your friends are great. Especially that Pinky. She and I had all kinds of fun bashing those aliens. But the truth is, I'm an old woman. Don't let all my hardware fool you—I'd rather be baking and playing canasta than just about anything else. It's nothing you've done—it's just that when you get to a certain age, you know what you like, and you know your time is limited, and you want to do the things you like as much as you can. So don't take it personally."

"Nana, are you giving me the 'it's not you, it's me' speech?" I stare at her.

"Well, honey, it's just that you've been awfully clingy. Always inviting me to eat with you, or go for a walk, or watch one of those dreadful robot westerns of yours. I get bored."

Wow. What do I say to that?

She pats me on the cheek. "Aw, you look sad now. Tell you what. This game's just wrapping up, so how about I come do whatever it was you wanted me to do? Eat some food with spoons or something, just the way you like."

Now she's pitying me. Great.

"Actually, I was going to ask you if you wanted to help Pinky and me put up some holiday decorations."

"That actually sounds fun." Nana perks up. "Okay, let me collect my money from these losers and we can be on our way."

My nana, the card shark. Or cardsharp, depending on what part of the universe you're from. Either way, my canasta-savvy grandmother really cleans up.

The elderly people retreating from her room don't seem to mind that they've just lost their money to her. They ask her to make sure she tells them about the next game before they shuffle away for their midmorning nap.

"I wouldn't have thought there would be such a big canasta following here," I say as we stroll back to the spot I left Pinky.

"Oh, it's everywhere," Nana says. "Canasta's highly addictive to old people. You youngsters have your bongs and injectables, but for us old people, canasta's the biggest high. Once someone starts, they can't stop."

"Are you teasing me, Nana?"

She stops, forcing me to stop, too. "I never joke about canasta."

"Right," I say. "Sorry. I guess I should stay away from it."

"Oh, you don't have to worry about it until your mid-fifties or so. Young people like you are immune."

We turn a corner, but Pinky isn't where I left her.

"It looks nice here." Nana pokes at a pom pom.

"Pinky must have moved on to another area. This is where she was when I came to check on you."

"Let's find her, then! We'll decorate this whole ship." Nana straightens her frumpy sweater, and I can tell she's fired up.

Maybe it's all that canasta in her system.

We find Pinky on the opposite side of the ship.

"Why are you all the way over here?" I ask. "I thought we were going to work from one end to the other."

Pinky ignores me. "Nana Rose! Good to see you out and about. You doing okay? Charlie was worried about you."

Pinky fist bumps Nana and they do some kind of secret handshake thing.

That's new.

"I'm fine, honey," Nana says. "Just needed some time with people my own age. You know how it is."

"Sure," Pinky agrees. "You old folks have to talk about the olden days, like when people liked to eat bologna."

"Pinky," I say, "I think you're being a little insensitive. No one on Earth has ever liked bologna."

Nana nods in confirmation.

Pinky looks amazed. "Really? Well, they love it on Abundance."

"Where?" I glance at Nana to see if she knows what Pinky's talking about, but she's wearing a blank expression.

"Abundance," Pinky repeats. "Don't let the name fool you. It's a smarmy little dustball of a planet. Exists entirely as a junk mail hub. I hate those guys."

"There's a whole planet for junk mail?" I learn something new every day.

"Oh yeah," Pinky affirms. "There has to be. Those jerks have been run off of all the decent planets. People can only take so many phishing scams and implications that their body parts aren't big enough before the people rise up and squash that shit."

"Makes sense. So, why are we on this side of the ship now?" I hope she'll answer me this time.

"I thought I heard something, but it must have been paranoia. We can get started over here. You two hang out for a minute and I'll bring the decorations."

Nana instead follows Pinky as she moves away. "I'll come

help. We should bring a lot of stuff. It's going to take a lot to cover up all this ship's ugly."

Few people could get away with insulting Pinky's home. Actually, probably just one person.

Then they're gone and I'm standing around in a hallway like a stalker or something. Awesome.

"Charlie!" I turn and there's Greta, smiling and radiant.

"Hey! Did Pinky call you?"

"Yes, early this morning, but I had to work. A group of executives got on board at the International Space Station, and I had to give them the Chance Fleet spiel. But I'm here now. Where are the decorations?"

"We did one hall, now we're going to work over here. Nana and Pinky went to get the stuff."

"Oh, okay." She smiles. "I guess we just wait?"

"Looks like it." A fiendish part of my brain recognizes that this is an opportunity to press her for information so I can get her the perfect present. "Is there anything in particular you like about Alpha Centauri? This will be my first time there."

She scrunches up her face in that way she does when she's thinking, which looks like she smells something bad. It's cute, though.

"Alpha Centauri is okay," she finally says. "It has a bunch of planets, lots of people, and there are things to do."

"But?" I prompt.

"I don't know, I just can't think of anything great about it. Or terrible, either. It's just kind of average."

That's not helpful.

"So there's nothing you suggest we do when we get there?" We've made a habit of visiting the various ports during stops and layovers, but she's not making this sound good.

"There are places we could go, if you want to."

"But nowhere that you really like."

She lets out a little sigh. "No, not really. I'm sorry."

"Don't be sorry. If there's nothing worth doing, we'll skip it. We only have a few ports there, anyway. We can stay on the ship and plan some fun for when we get to the Mebdarian system. I cannot wait to see that."

She brightens. "Ooh, yes, that's a good one. Lots of fun stuff to do."

"Think Pinky will show us around her home planet? I did show you guys a little bit of Earth, so it seems fair."

"I don't know. She's never said much about her home."

"Like someone else I know," I tease.

She's about to say something when her gaze shifts. "There they are. Wow, that's a lot of stuff."

Indeed, all I really see is a mass of boxes and bags with two pairs of legs underneath. It's kind of funny looking, like all the stuff has grown its own legs.

"Where did you get all this?" Greta asks when they set the boxes down. She's already rummaging around.

She pulls a long pike out of a box. It's topped with a red gumdrop that's bigger than my fist. "Hey, does this—" she breaks off when the gumdrop lights up.

"We found a bunch of stuff hidden in the back of the storage room." Pinky sets down her mountain of festive goods.

"Awesome!" Greta begins digging out other pikes and setting them in a pile. Some have gumdrops of other colors, while others have snowmen or demented little clowns with tall hats. "These are great! We can put them all down the hall."

Pinky's pulling green and red stockings out of the box she'd carried. "There are hundreds of these. We could put one on every cabin door, probably."

Nana's rummaging around now too, so I lean over the box she carried and pull out a rubber mask. I don't know what it's meant to celebrate, but it's ugly and warty and I put it aside. Then I find something really good.

"Look at this! It's a snap-together sleigh, with a seat people could actually sit on. I wonder where we could put that."

Greta comes over and peers in at it. "Maybe the dining room? It definitely wouldn't fit in a corridor."

"I wonder if there are any reindeer that go with it." I move some things aside and dig deeper. A sound makes me pull back.

"What's wrong?" Greta asks.

I laugh at myself. "Nothing. It's just jingle bells." I pull out a basket full of bells the size of ping pong balls. "For a second there, the sound reminded me of—"

I freeze when a blagrook head raises up and looks at me.

"Bloody hell, it's a blagrook!" Pinky reaches down, grabs a gumdrop pike, and swings it baseball style, knocking the creature against the wall with a hard crack.

Greta's glow is entirely gone, but her jaw is set as she grabs a big pink gumdrop pike. "There's never just one of them."

All of our eyes are fixed on the boxes.

Nana circles around behind. "You all ready?"

Crap crap crap crap crap. Am I ready to face a bunch of bloodthirsty blagrooks that are about to get dumped out of holiday bins? This is like some horror movie.

I bend down and grab a gumdrop pole. "Let's do it."

Nana shoves the boxes over in one movement and a dozen or more writhing, flailing blagrooks roll out.

Pinky's on it, assuming the first line of defense. She knocks three of them flying before they even get to their feet.

Nana's grabs one with her bare hands and cracks its head against the wall. And then another.

Greta holds her ground when one comes running for her. With a grunt, she swings her gumdrop stick. The blagrook hits the wall, but much more softly than when Pinky does it.

Fortunately, Pinky steps on it while it's dazed.

I hold my ground, too, waiting for one of the things to come my way. But they don't. The three women in my life have this situation in hand. While they're murdering blagrooks, the cabin doors start fluttering open.

It's kind of funny, actually. A door will open, a head pops out, a person gasps or screams, and the door shuts again. And then it happens again with another door.

I can't help it. I start laughing.

Greta looks at me like I'm nuts, then she starts to giggle, too. Soon, Nana and Pinky are laughing too, even as they're all pounding mean little aliens.

"Ha ha ha!" Pinky shouts, bashing one against the wall so hard it leaves a grease stain behind.

"That's ho ho ho," I remind her.

"Right. Dammit. I keep messing that one up."

When none of the little demons are moving, we stand, poised and ready, but it appears we've gotten them all.

Well, they've gotten them all.

Nana gives one of the boxes a good shake, then does the same with the other. Rolls of ribbon and boxes of balloons shift and tumble out, but no more blagrooks.

Gus comes running around the corner, carrying a pulse rifle. "Clear the way!"

We stand still.

He stops, scans the scene, and stands there awkwardly. "There were guest complaints about a blagrook invasion."

"We got it," Pinky says. "No sweat."

"Oh. Well. Thanks." Gus seems unsure of what to do next, and I understand. What does one do with a dozen blagrook carcasses, and a couple metric tons of holiday decorations?

That's nobody's idea of a good time.

Gus gathers himself. "Right. Pinky and Mrs. Cyborg, could you please remain here to reassure guests that the situation is under control?"

"I prefer Ms. Cyborg, if you're going to be racist," Nana sniffs.

"Of course," he answers smoothly. "My apologies, Ms. Cyborg.

Greta, it will be up to you to make people feel comfortable. I'll organize the porters to clean up and finish putting up these decorations."

"What about me?" I ask.

He blinks, as if seeing me for the first time. "Oh, hello, Mr. Kenny."

"Aw, come on, dude. I've been here the whole time," I protest. "When you tell this story, don't leave me out of it."

"My grandson was the one who first found the vile monsters," Nana says, stepping toward Gus.

"He did!" Pinky steps in, too, still holding her gumdrop cudgel. "In fact, if it weren't for Charlie and his plague of bad luck, I bet these things wouldn't even be on the ship."

"Uh, that's probably not a good thing to tell people," I say. I know she's trying to be supportive, but that doesn't make me sound good.

Greta moves in, too, and they're so busy defending me that none of them see the lone blagrook that tumbles out of a box when something shifts.

I don't even scream, and I'm feeling really proud of myself for that, but it bares its fangs and hisses. The only way I'm not getting my jugular ripped out is if I handle this myself.

All right. I can do this. I'm ready. I choke up on my gumdrop stake, which I've continued to clutch—I mean hold. I've been holding it in a manly way.

Resisting the urge to close my eyes to protect them from the sharp claws of the monster, I stare right at it and swing.

Hard.

It flies, just like when Pinky hits them, and falls to the ground motionless. Just like when Pinky does it.

Oh my god.

Oh my god, I did it.

Now Greta and Nana are hugging me and Pinky's making sure

the thing is dead and all the blood in my entire body is rushing to my head.

"You saw it!" I shout at Gus. I didn't mean to say that. Or to yell.

Gus locks eyes with me, and for a moment, we're having a whole man-to-man, I-see-what-you-did-there moment.

Then his professionalism slides into place and he's regular old Gus again. "Yes, sir. I did indeed see that. Now if you'll excuse me, I need to see about handling this mess. We can't have the passengers seeing this."

Pinky uses the hooked part of a giant candy cane to push all the dead blagrooks into a pile. That's nice of her, simplifying the unpleasant task that lies ahead of the porters.

"You did good, Charlie." Pinky gives me a high five. "Very heroic."

"Really?" I wonder if she's just humoring me.

"Couldn't have done it better myself."

I tuck away that sound bite in my memory because I'm pretty sure I'll never hear her say it again.

Then Pinky lets out of regretful sigh.

"What's wrong?" I ask.

"Once Gus gets back, we're going to have to figure out how to get rid of the rest of the blagrooks." Pinky looks grim.

"You think there are more?" Nana asks. "I haven't heard any."

"There's almost no chance of these being the only ones," Pinky says.

Greta takes a deep breath and sets her jaw. "Okay, then. Let's figure out how to get rid of them, without letting the guests know. We can't have a panic. It would scare people away from flying on the Chance Fleet."

"That's what Gus would say," Pinky says. "But I don't have to be mad at him anymore. He gave me a really nice apology and a sweet I-heart-flamingoes t-shirt that fits great."

"Wait," I say. "Why would he have a shirt like that?"

Pinky shrugs. "He was planning to give me an early Hannukah present? I can't imagine he knows anyone else my size who loves flamingoes."

"Yeah. See, he must really like you." I try to say this convincingly.

Pinky continues to look indifferent. "Hm, that might explain a thing or two. But let's focus on what's important here. We need to get rid of those blagrooks."

I hide an inward sigh. I didn't get even five minutes to celebrate my victory. But no matter. I need to help Greta and Pinky figure this out, because this isn't just Greta's employment we're talking about.

It's our home.

4

"WHAT ATTRACTS BLAGROOKS?" I ask.

The four of us have gathered in Nana's cabin, which, fortunately, is bigger than mine.

"Warmth, noise, and blood." Pinky's answer comes immediately.

"What kind of blood?" Greta asks. "The spilled kind, or the stuff that's still inside us?"

"Both. They're not picky. Though the spilled kind has a stronger odor they can smell from farther away."

Greta nods. "Okay, then. We'll throw a party."

Nana's been sitting in the corner, leaning back with her eyes closed. I'm pretty sure she was napping. But she straightens and her eyes open. "You're going to use your guests as bait? I like it."

"Not bait." Greta cringes. "At least, not exactly. I mean, how better to keep passengers safe from blagrooks than get them all together where we can guard them? But if that also draws the demons out so we can eradicate them, then that's all the better, right?"

We all look to Pinky because, let's face it, when it comes to battle, she's our general.

"It could work." She frowns deeply, her eyes making tiny but quick movements from side to side as she thinks. "Yeah, I could make it work. But it won't be easy to plan a party on short notice and get everyone to attend."

Greta bounces up to her feet. "Leave that to me! I'll organize the porters, draft the maintenance workers, and fill Gus in on what's happening. You three figure out the plan for the blagrooks."

She hurries out.

"Think she can do it?" Nana asks.

"Absolutely." There's no doubt in my mind. If Greta decided to move a mountain, it would happen, one way or another. I have absolute faith in her. It's not just about her luck, either. It's also her heart, her kindness, and her tenacity.

"Are you thinking what I'm thinking, Pinky?"

Pinky slaps her knee. "Yes! We are going to do this! I've got it all planned out. I just need to know one thing."

She turns to my nana. "How dependent are you on oxygen?"

I DON'T KNOW how Greta has done it, but the secondary loading bay has become a holiday wonderland.

Twinkling lights provide just the right amount of light in a room festooned with a hodgepodge of decorations so bizarre that it's somehow harmonious.

Porters expertly work the room with trays of drinks. Pinky's provided everything from basic party punch to what she calls a Wham Bam Slammer. I haven't tasted one because I need to remain alert, but it smells like pine and gin.

I don't think I'd want one of those anyway.

Instead, I accept a cup of non-alcoholic punch as I wander the room. People are having a wonderful time. Most have dressed up in colorful clothes and some folks dance at the end of the loading bay that's been miraculously transformed into a dance floor. It has strobe lights and everything.

Greta is amazing. It's only been two hours since I whacked that blagrook.

Did you think I wasn't going to bring that up as much as possible? Because I am. It doesn't even need to fit in anywhere. I'm just going to mention it anyway, from time to time.

Anyway, my real job is to keep an eye out for anything weird, either from the guests or anything else. As a group, we figured that if anything weird was going to happen, I'd be the one to detect it.

I'm at one with embracing the reality of my...well, let's call it a nonconformity. What makes me a little nervous, though, is that Nana's a Kenny, too, under that cybernetic gear, and she's the critical bit in this plan. I'm not sure how much of the redshirt bad luck she still has, and it's a real question mark in this venture.

Greta promised me this would all work, though. Some people believe in angels or flying reindeer or talking wheels of cheese, but I believe in Greta Saltz. I'm putting everything in her hands because she is my miracle.

I sidle by Nana, who's being aggressively cyborg. Whenever someone walks into the zone she's protecting, she reaches for them and starts saying a lot of things about assimilation and joining the union.

It's working great. Nobody is going into the target zone.

"How's it going, Nana?"

"Fine, Charlie. I'm having fun. Best party I've been to in a while."

I think she's serious. "Does it ever bother you when people are afraid of you or if they say mean things about you being a cyborg?"

"Nah. When you're as old as I am, you see how little all that matters. They're the ones with the problem, not me."

"I hope I get to be that old. I mean, without becoming a cyborg. No offense."

"You'll get there, I think," she says. "You've got Pinky and Greta. You really lucked out. I'm not surprised, either. Of all my grandkids, you were always my favorite."

"Really?" I'm completely surprised to hear that.

"Well, no. But several have met their natural fate, and Benny always stole from me. So you weren't always my favorite, but you're my favorite now."

"Oh. Well, I guess that's still kind of good."

"Sure it is!" she insists. "Life is for the living and we, my boy, are living."

"We are."

Nana says, "I was talking to Gus, and he tells me he's been thinking of retiring on Mebdar IV."

I raise my eyebrows. "Is he still upset? I thought he'd be doing better now, with the elevator fixed."

"I don't know. I think apologizing to Pinky broke something in him, even though she went easy on him, in my opinion. She didn't even hit him. But he's not sure if he wants to keep dealing with customer complaints and all the hassles of pleasing people. So I thought I might check out the Mebdarian system with him. He tells me there's a wicked canasta community there. I could really clean up."

"Are you sure a retirement planet won't be too boring for you?" I can't imagine her there.

"I'm not sure. But I can take a little vacation. Try it out. See if it fits."

"Sure, that makes sense. I could take a look at it with you, if you like." Though it's been nice having her on board, now that she's stopped breaking into my cabin and trying to assimilate me, she won't be happy here long-term. I'd like to see her find someplace she really likes.

She pats my cheek. "Such a good boy."

She tilts her head to the side. “I hear them. Stay alert, boy. It’s about to go down.”

“Right.” I feel awkward, but I kind of want to hug her. Just in case things don’t go according to plan.

Nana rolls her eyes at me. “I’m not gonna die! Get out of here!”

Okay, so much for that. I get out of the danger zone. I look up at the hatch above, where Pinky has put a bolus of blood from the medbay to make sure that none of the blagrooks can resist.

Greta’s voice comes over the intercom. “Hi, everyone, and thank you for coming to our holiday celebration. We are so touched that you’ve chosen us to take you to your loved ones during this time of togetherness. Right now, we’re going to do the traditional Cringaloo countdown, which signifies the end of one season and the beginning of the next. If you’d like to join in, feel free, and it’s customary to celebrate by hugging someone or throwing confetti. But do whatever you’re comfortable with. Happy Cringaloo!”

I don’t know what this Cringaloo is, but it seems a lot like a New Year’s celebration to me, which made it perfect for our plan.

Greta remains at the microphone and begins counting down. “Ten…nine…eight…”

I look around, but don’t see Pinky. I know she’s there, though. Somewhere.

Nana’s poised for action.

“Five…four…”

I hope this works. I hold my breath.

“Two…one! Happy Cringaloo!”

The hatch above opens, raining blagrooks like confetti down toward Nana. She hits the containment panel and clear walls snap into place around her.

Everyone’s hugging and throwing confetti and it’s really hard to hear or see, but my attention doesn’t waver from Nana grabbing onto a floor hitch as the air lock opens.

She's wrenched off her feet as the blagrooks go flying into space. It only takes ten seconds, but it feels like forever, watching her hang on with her body being sucked toward the great abyss.

Then the air lock closes and Pinky drops down from the hatch, helping Nana up.

A piece of confetti hits me in the eye because of course it did, but I barely notice.

It worked.

I hurry over to Nana and Pinky. "Was that all of them? Are you sure?"

"Yep," Pinky says. "They flock together. There's no way any of them could resist all this. They're really stupid."

"Well, they're dead now."

"Actually, no." Pinky shakes her head. "They can do fine in space. They join together into a bunch and just float. Guarantee you they'll make it to Abundance."

"The junk mail planet?"

"That's the one."

I feel good about this poetic justice. "Are you okay, Nana?"

She smiles. "Just fine. My back cracked while I was hanging on, and fixed a joint that's been bothering me. I feel great! Now, where's that Gus? I wanted to talk to him about our trip to Mebdar IV."

"Nana Rose is hanging out with Gus now?" Pinky purses her lips thoughtfully.

"I think they're going to tear up the canasta circuit or something. Does this mean you'll be nicer to Gus?"

Pinky shrugs. "He apologized, so we're as good as we ever were. But if Nana Rose likes him, there must be something worthwhile about him."

"I guess so. I want her to be happy." I look around the room at all the happy, celebratory people. "I can't believe we pulled this off."

Pinky smiles.

I'm a little surprised. Pinky doesn't smile much.

"It's been a good year," she says. "We've had some great adventures, and I got to hunt blagrooks twice and become a movie star."

She pats my shoulder. "Thanks, Charlie."

"Why are you thanking me?"

"Because none of it would have happened if you hadn't come aboard. Let's keep having fun, huh?"

I feel all warm and fuzzy inside. "I can't think of anything I'd rather do."

"I can." She hitches her thumb at the dance floor. "See you later."

I turn, and Greta's there. Smiling and radiant, and looking like the greatest thing I've ever seen in my life.

"You arranged an amazing party," I say. "I can't believe you managed this in two hours."

She laughs. "It took a little work, but I think it worked out."

"You've made the perfect holiday."

"Have I?"

"Pinky got to whack blagrooks, and Nana got to save the day in a way that redshirts never do. She's probably going to tear up the canasta circuit on Mebdar IV, too. I was worried about getting them presents, but what could I give them that could top that?"

Greta laughs. "I've been trying to figure out the right presents for everyone, too, but nothing seemed right. Especially for you. It's not like you care about owning a lot of things."

"In my cabin?" I joke. "Where would I put it?"

"I think I just thought of the perfect thing for us to give each other, though." Her eyes sparkle.

Not literally. I mean, her skin does literally luminesce, but her eyes aren't actually metallic or anything. I'm speaking figuratively.

"Blagrook-beating gumdrop bats?" I guess.

She giggles. "No. Look." She points up.

Mistletoe.

"You found tree fungus," I say, in the stupidest response to a girl that any guy has ever had.

"I was hoping we could do that Earth tradition you were telling me about." Her glow increases, and I realize she's blushing.

Hesitantly, not quite believing this is happening, I put my arms around her. She steps closer and puts her hands on my shoulders.

Then the most magical thing that has ever happened in my whole life happens.

The holidays aren't about things we buy for one another. They're about being with the people who matter, sharing our hearts, and making the moments count.

And, maybe, just a little bit of blagrook bashing.

Because I really did smash that one. You saw it.

Now avert your eyes. I have some Greta-smooching to do.

RIDING THE WARRIOR CHICKEN BUS IN THE LAND OF DANCE BATTLES

5

I KISSED GRETA SALTZ, and I liked it.

Of course I liked it. I love her, and she's the most amazing person in the universe. And now, I am completely certain she likes me, at least somewhat. A nice girl like Greta doesn't kiss just any schmo who comes along.

Just this particular schmo.

I know what you're thinking. I can practically hear it. *Charlie, of course she likes you! She returns your feelings! It's so obvious! Have you even read this story?*

I assure you, my conservative approach to the estimation of Greta's feelings for me is not dramatic license. I'm not drawing out the plot here.

In spite of my recent successes, particularly in the area of not dying, I am still, at the most basic level, a redshirt. There's no changing that. So regardless of the run of adventure I've had in the past several months, it doesn't change my DNA.

Once a redshirt, always a redshirt. And do you know what the spouses of redshirts become?

Widows, widowers, and collateral damage.

So even though I adore her, and I'm pretty sure she's fond of me, I'm not exactly eager to take those final steps into a full-on relationship that leads to marriage.

I don't want to doom the woman I love.

As such, I'm satisfied to live in a flux of ambiguity. Does she love me? I don't know. Is this going somewhere? Seems unlikely. What does the future hold?

Me, getting disemboweled by a laser pointer, maybe. Or some other seemingly unlikely demise.

I'm not so naïve as to think that Greta and Pinky can stave off my fate forever. It's always been a foregone conclusion—a statistical certainty. As such, each day is a gift, and I take them as they come, without thinking ahead long-term.

In the short term, I have a visit to the Mebdarian system to look forward to. First, we're hitting Pinky's homeworld of Mebdar II, then we'll visit Mebdar IV, retirement haven for the elderly.

Nana is getting more and more excited about it the closer we get. She and Gus are going to have a good look-see, and I am absolutely certain that Nana's got her fingers crossed that Mebdar IV will be a hotbed of canasta action.

I've caught her working her canasta hustle on other passengers of the *Second Chance* on three occasions now, in complete violation of interstellar law. I hope she can satisfy her canasta fix before she lands herself in jail.

She was never such a rebel before the cyborgs assimilated her.

I've been on board the *Second Chance* for eight months now, and I've settled into a happy little routine.

Yes, I'm still a creature of habit. Routine gives me comfort. Even if I had woken up this morning with Greta's luck, I'd probably still be rife with paranoia and unease.

As I step up to my storage compartment, I try to imagine having her luck. It would be fantastic. All of the ridiculous things that have happened to my family members would cease to exist for me.

On the other hand, if I'd been born with Greta's luck, she'd have found me dull as dirt rather than the harbinger-of-excitement vibe I have going for me now.

Funny to think of it like that. In a weird way, my bad luck turned into good fortune.

This epiphany is almost enough to make me give that red shirt at the bottom of my clothing pile a good, hard looking at. There it is, resting like a siren alert in all its crimson glory among my beige and off-white clothing. I stare at it, wondering if today should be the day I put it on.

A strange feeling creeps over me. Kind of like when you're in a swimming pool and you step into a spot that's suddenly, suspiciously warm. It's a sense that something terrible has happened and you're right smack in the middle of it.

I feel like the shirt is looking back at me.

I grab my trusty beige clothes and slam the storage compartment closed.

Not today.

If you think about it, just considering wearing the shirt is a bit of a victory.

If you think about it really hard. Sort of. In a way.

Whatever.

After I'm dressed and ready to face whatever this day is going to bring, I go to Pinky's bar to help with the morning rush of drinks.

Isn't it funny how judgmental people can be about drinking in the morning, except in the case of certain drinks?

Down a glass of wine in the morning and people will label you as someone who has a problem. Drop some champagne into a little orange juice and make a mimosa, and you're just being social.

Nobody knows why.

Of course, on the *Second Chance*, we have more than bellinis, mimosas, and Bloody Marys. We also have Morning Wakeups, Cheerful Seagulls, and Sunrise Mass Murders.

That last one is one of Pinky's creations. Don't ask. I sure never have. It seems like it would be unwise to do so, just in case it's a somewhat autobiographical kind of beverage.

"Hey, Pinky."

Usually, when I greet Pinky in the morning, she slams a freshly made drink on the counter and says hello. Or something similar to hello. At the very least, she grunts.

Today, she turns around slowly, then her shoulders slump. She leans forward with her elbows on the bar and sighs.

Oh, shit.

This has got to be bad. I've never seen Pinky approach any situation with anything less than utmost confidence and certainy.

"I'll get Greta." When *kenogu* brings something bad, Greta is the antidote.

Pinky sighs again and straightens. "Don't bother her. She'll get here when she gets here."

"But..." I'm in a pickle. I don't know how to describe her current state of dejection without it sounding unflattering and possibly prompting her to pound me into jelly. I skip over that and go straight to, "What's wrong?"

"My brother wants to get married." Pinky says this with the same tone that one would use to say, *I have severe poisoning and only hours to live,* or, *having children is definitely no longer in my future.*

You might think those are odd phrases, but you'd be surprised how often they've come up in the Kenny family.

"And..." I try to come up with a reason she'd be so morose about her brother's upcoming nuptials. "You don't like his betrothed?"

"Be-what?" She squints at me. "Is that a human anatomical part or something? Because Mebdarian don't have 'em."

"Uh, no, it means the person he's engaged to. The one he's going to marry."

"I haven't met her yet."

I pause. "So you're concerned she won't be good enough for him? Surely, if he likes her, that's all that matters."

"He hasn't met her yet, either." Pinky comes around the bar and sits on a stool.

Wow, she's really upset. I've never seen her do that.

"How's he going to get married if he doesn't even have a girlfriend?" I'm confused. This isn't new. It's just annoying.

"I'm the noona. The older sister. For Mebdarians, that means that it's my job to find him a wife." Pinky runs a hand through her blue-black hair.

The pieces start to fall into place. "Ohh, so he wants you to find him a girl. And you don't want to."

"It's not that I don't want to," Pinky retorts. "Having him happily settled would be one less thing for me to worry about. Our parents have been gone for a while now, so it's been my job to make sure he's doing okay. It's a lot of responsibility."

"Oh, I didn't realize your parents had passed away."

"Who said they died?" She stares at me like I'm an idiot. "I said they're gone. They bought a galaxy hopper and just float around from port to port, eating chocolate snack foods and playing terrible music."

"That sounds very adventurous. I've never known anyone who did that."

She shrugs. "It's not adventurous, really. One hopper dock looks much like the next one. Old people in folding chairs, eating canned goods and complaining about their kids and grandkids. Sometimes they even travel in little gangs from one place to the next."

That does sound a lot less exciting than the mental picture I had. But we've drifted off topic, and I try to steer us back on course. "Okay, so you have to find your brother a girl."

"Yeah." Pinky sounds downright blue.

"I guess that's what we can do when we visit your homeworld, instead of sightseeing. Unless sightseeing is a way to pick up eligible women to set up with your brother." Since I know so little about native Mebdarian culture, I'm trying not to make assumptions.

"I wish it could be that easy." Pinky grimaces.

"Well," I say, "why can't it be? We'll take Greta. Surely that will work."

Pinky straightens and she looks thoughtful. "True. But you're coming too, right? I mean, no offense, but you're not exactly a good-luck charm, and I'd rather my brother doesn't accidentally fall in love with a shoe or something."

"Hey," I say, not really offended, but feeling like I should defend myself. "Nothing like that has ever happened. Usually it's just, you know, life-threatening stuff."

Pinky rubs her chin. "Well...I guess you can come. Just try not to screw things up."

"I always *try* not to."

"Yeah." She gets to her feet. Hopefully this is a good sign. "I know. It's not your fault, Charlie." She takes a deep breath. "It'll be fine. We'll find my brother someone nice, and then I can check that off my list of things I have to accomplish."

"It'll be great." I try to sound enthusiastic, but really, the idea of matchmaking is entirely foreign to me. Who would put that kind of thing in my hands? No one, that's who. "So why is it the older sister's job to find a wife for the younger brother?"

"Statistics."

This, of course, interests me tremendously. Statistics are my jam. "Why's that?"

"The Mebdarian divorce rate used to be crazy. Ninety percent of all couples who married ended up divorcing. And that's bad for the economy. So about three hundred years ago, we set out to find a way to improve the likelihood of marriage success. We tried lots of things, but in the end, marriages that started with the older sister setting someone up were thirty times more likely to succeed. So that became the thing everyone wanted to do. And by now, it's tradition."

"That sounds pretty legit to me. What a logical way to handle a problem."

Pinky nods. "We're a logical people. That's why so many things were invented by Mebdarians."

"Oh. Uh, right." I nod agreeably.

She looks at the list of pending drink orders, which must have been piling up during her time of angst.

"Want some help with those?" I ask.

"Sure. You can handle the alcoholic ones. I'll get the rest."

"Okay." I move around the bar to begin mixing drinks. I don't ask her why she chose this method of splitting the orders. Presumably, part of it is that there are far fewer alcoholic drinks in the queue. The other part, whatever it is, is probably insulting, and I've learned to quit while I'm ahead when it comes to asking Pinky leading questions.

It's just not good for my ego.

An hour later, Greta arrives, and we fill her in on Pinky's family situation.

"Wow! I've never done any matchmaking, much less on someone else's planet. This should be interesting." She begins to tear apart her lushfruit muffin, then pauses. She carefully picks it up and takes a bite instead.

She's getting good at that.

"What kind of woman do you think he'd be interested in?" Greta asks. "That might help us know where to look."

"That's a good idea," Pinky says thoughtfully. She leans against the bar and puts her hand to her chin in contemplation.

She looks quite regal this way. You know, if the royalty in question has twenty-inch biceps.

"Smart," Pinky decides. "But not too smart. And pretty. But

not vain about it. He wouldn't like the kind of girl who takes an hour to get ready to go somewhere."

"Low-maintenance, then," I say.

"No," she says emphatically. "No maintenance. A cyborg would be all wrong for him. I mean, I like Nana Rose heaps, but he'll definitely want a girl with all her biological parts. If ya know what I mean." She gives me a point and a wink.

I don't know why, but whenever Pinky makes a sexual reference, I feel a deep sense of discomfort. Kind of like the feeling you'd get imagining Santa Claus getting freaky. Some things just don't belong in the same context.

I try not to show it, though. "That's not what I meant. I meant a girl who's easygoing and not fussy. A go-with-the-flow type."

"Ohh." Pinky nods. "I gotcha. Yeah. Like that."

"Does he have any particular interests?" Greta asks. "Something that would be nice for them to have in common?"

"Particular?" Pinky presses her lips together. "Hm. Jon likes lightstream comics, casual dining, and improv dance battles. His turn-ons include sandy beaches, the smell of fresh oranges, and girls with a sense of humor. How's that?"

I'm not sure which item to address first. As usual, Pinky has steered the conversation in a strange direction.

Greta wears an expression like she's just sat on a wet sponge, so I know she feels the same way I do.

"Uhm," she says, "are you writing up a dating profile for him?"

Pinky shakes her head. "No way. No brother of mine is going to find his future wife by submitting an application. We'll do it the right way, with me finding her for him."

I'm not really sure that's better, but if it's the Mebdarian way, then I guess, for them, it is. It does have the backing of statistical research, which gives me confidence.

I say, "Okay. So why did that sound like a dating profile?"

She shrugs. "Just trying to make it sound snappy. You know, so

I have a good sound bite ready for when I'm selling him to some unsuspecting woman."

I fear for poor Jon and his chances of matrimony. I sense that Pinky lacks a certain subtlety that's probably required for this endeavor.

"Okay…" Greta says, "so what's this about his turn-ons? Isn't that a little…odd for a sister to mention?"

"And what's up with the smell of oranges?" I add. On the list of things to unpack from Pinky's prior statement, this is minor, but it's going to bother me if I don't ask. You know how sometimes when you go to bed, you aren't thinking about something, but as soon as you lie down, something from the day just gets into your head and won't get out? This is going to be one of those things. I can tell.

"Oh, I made that up," Pinky says. "I just think it will play well. I mean, who doesn't like the scent of oranges? And it makes him sound sensitive, I think."

I'm not so sure of that. "So you made up the thing about dance battles too?"

"Oh, hell no." Pinky's eyes widen in a look of sudden passion. "Dance battles are the official planetary pastime of Mebdar II. He and I are one badass team. Nobody beats us. Well, except that one time when we were up against a pair of galactic pro dancers. It was lame of them to even engage in a dance battle. But we still beat them, afterward, if you know what I mean." She laughs heartily.

Greta and I exchange a look. It's the kind of look where two people try to communicate a long string of exclamation marks using only their eyes.

Once again, I feel like I'm at the shallow end of a pool, trying to find the right place to wade in and hoping not to find any warm spots.

"Okay, so…planetary pastime, huh?" I say casually. As if such a thing is normal.

"You didn't know that?" Pinky stares at me like I'm a bug in a jar.

I shake my head. Does this make me a sectarian rube?

"You knew it, right?" Pinky asks Greta.

"Uh, no, actually." Greta ducks her head.

Whew. Guess I'm not such a rube.

"How can you not know that?" Pinky asks.

"Well," Greta ventures, "it's not like I've ever seen you engage in a dance battle. I've never seen anyone do it, actually."

"Oh, dance battles never happen on ships. It's a rule."

Sure. Of course it is. Because that makes complete sense. When dancing at someone—and having them dance back—is a way to assert your dominance, of *course* it can't happen in space.

Makes sense, right?

And if you said *yes* to that, could you please explain it to me?

Pinky only tolerates so many questions before she gets pissy, so I need to pick and choose carefully at this point.

"So, in these battles," I say slowly, "do you ever actually hit the other people, or is it strictly about busting moves?"

Pinky looks at me then. It's a look that's part disdain and part pity, sprinkled with just a hint of ridicule.

Right. That's my cue. "Well, I should get to work. I have lots of numbers to crunch today!"

I sound overly enthusiastic, and I know it, but there's no going back now.

"Anything interesting today?" Greta asks.

"The eating habits of twenty-two to twenty-six year olds."

"Oh. Well, I'm sure that's interesting to someone." Greta shrugs.

Pinky has begun wiping down the bar, and I decide it's the perfect moment to make my escape. Maybe Greta can get some good info in my absence.

I know that sounds cowardly, but it's not. Without my luck

counteracting hers, she's more likely to get somewhere. It's not cowardliness, it's pragmatism.

Besides, I really do have work to take care of.

"I'll catch you two later," I say.

"We dock at Mebar II in a day and a half," Pinky says. "You should probably do some extra research on the place. You know, for safety."

Well, that's nice. She's concerned for my well-being.

Then she adds, "And also so you don't embarrass me by doing something really dumb."

And there it is. Another crushing mic drop from Pinky.

Right. Off to my room I go to get some work done.

6

SINCE I'LL BE SPENDING the next couple days on Mebdar II, I'll check in with Nana in the morning before we go.

Overall, Nana has done a great job of adjusting to life in space. Being a cyborg has really made her adaptable. She's even stopped trying to assimilate me while I'm sleeping, and I can't tell you how grateful I am for that.

"Would you want to join us on the planet?" I ask her. I've visited her cabin, which is almost exactly like mine, except she has cans of DW-101 everywhere. It's her industrial lubricant of choice, and she says it makes her joints feel great.

Nana's sliding her feet into a pair of house slippers. She's taken to thinking of the *Second Chance* as her house and as such, she's decided that she need only wear house shoes while on board. I can't fault her logic, but it is kind of funny to see an elderly cyborg walking the corridors in her slippers.

"As much as I'd enjoy a chance to hang out with Pinky, I'm going to have to say no." Nana pats me on the shoulder in consolation.

I could mention the fact that she could go along to hang out with her grandson, but I don't. There's no point. She likes Pinky better. I get it.

I'd like her better, too.

"But why?" I ask. "There's nothing going on here."

"That's what you think." There's a certain gleam in her eye—the real one, not the red, glowing one—and I know she's up to something.

"Are you planning some kind of big canasta shakedown? I keep telling you, you're going to get into some really big trouble."

"Of course not," she says soothingly. "Nothing of the sort. Some of us older passengers are going to have a screening party for some old movies, that's all."

Some people think cyborgs can't lie because of their programming. Those people are wrong.

But there's really nothing I can do about it. Nana's a grown woman of sound mind (the courts have ruled that simply being a cyborg doesn't imply a loss of sanity), and she's clearly not going to listen to me.

"It could be fun," I say. "Imagine the adventure we could have. There might even be dance battles."

Nana perks up. "Dance battles, you say?"

"Apparently, it's a planetary pastime."

Nana looks thoughtful. "I do like to bust some killer moves from time to time. I bet Pinky and I would make a fantastic dance team."

"So you'll come?" I ask hopefully. If she's on the planet, she can't be shaking down old people for their canasta money.

"Nah. Not today, anyway. Like I said, I've got plans. If I have time tomorrow, I'll see if I can come down and catch up with you kids."

I know it's the best offer she's going to make. "Okay. Just please stay out of trouble."

"Don't worry about it, Charlie." She pats me on the shoulder. "These bags of water have got nothing on me."

"Nana."

"What?"

I say, "I'm a bag of water, too. So are Pinky and Greta. It's not a nice thing to say."

"Whoops, didn't mean to say it out loud. It's usually a phrase we only use at the cyborg union meetings." She holds her arms up in an *oops* gesture.

"Okay..." I really don't know what else to say to that.

"I'll try to make it down. Maybe I can make some nice cookies for the girl you guys choose for Pinky's brother. They always say the best way to a woman's heart is through her gut."

No. No, they don't say that. Unless it's in a creepy, eat-your-organs horror movie. In any other scenario, literally no one ever says that.

Now I'm kind of hoping she doesn't join us on Mebdar II, because Nana's cookies aren't going to convince anyone to do anything but make a hasty retreat.

That's not what we'll be going for, and it definitely won't help us score Jon a wife.

So I bid Nana goodbye and resist the urge to admonish her again about illegal activities. If she hasn't listened by now, she never will.

7

As Pinky, Greta, and I board the elevator to go down to Mebdar II, I brace myself for whatever might happen next.

True to her word, Pinky has adjusted the *Chance 3000*. It only activates when there are no passengers aboard. That means Gus has enjoyed a reduction in stress level, because he's no longer fielding dozens of customer complaints every day. I don't think it's helped, though. Gus has been acting cracked for a while now.

The *Chance 3000* still treats the ship's crew to random shenanigans. Sometimes it's fun and sometimes it isn't. Pinky has programmed in a certain unpredictability that leaves you always holding your breath.

In a way, it's exciting. I guess.

I haven't gotten over my foreboding for random events, so I'm not feeling the happy-time vibe.

Greta, though, looks curious and ready for something to happen.

That's my Greta—she's not afraid of anything. I dig that about her.

State your desired destination.

It's a low-key start. Frankly, I'm underwhelmed. Which is good.

"Down," I say.

Descending.

We look at each other. Could it be this simple or is the *Chance 3000* lulling us into a false sense of safety?

Greta and I both look at Pinky. This is her creation, after all.

But Pinky shrugs. "I told you, I put in a lot of randomness. Sometimes this thing pulls off stuff that surprises me, too."

All we can do is wait.

Nothing happens.

This isn't unprecedented. A couple times, the *Chance 3000* gave us an entirely uneventful trip.

This must be one of those times.

About halfway down, I'm just breathing and minding my own business when at the very end of my inhale, I sense something amiss.

Maybe I imagined it.

No. No. I really didn't.

On my next breath of air, I'm suddenly in hell. A sulfuric stench has invaded my olfactory sense. The depth of the horrific, reeking nightmare is something I can't properly convey in words. I feel like I'm smothering, even as I'm breathing, and I try to hold my breath.

But that only makes my next breath even deeper and every part of my brain stops working except the part that's screaming, *Escape!*

With my hand over my face, I look at Pinky.

She shrugs. "Wasn't me."

She's playing it cool, like it doesn't bother her, but I can see her nostrils twitching. She has only herself to blame for this. Greta and I, on the other hand, have a very worthy target for our disgust.

Greta has never looked less luminescent. Her glow is gone. She looks quite ill. In fact, I think she might—

Even though I register the sudden rounding of her shoulders and back, I find myself unwilling to release my arm from around her waist. I don't want her to fall while she heaves her guts up, so I will weather the backsplash.

Then, my darling Greta is depositing her stomach contents on the floor of the elevator and, as it happens, our shoes.

As if the smell alone weren't enough to make me want to toss my cookies. Now I have the horrible sounds Greta's making in my ears, and I'm trying really hard not to look, even as I hold her up.

How long is this ride, anyway?

The doors finally open, and I help Greta stumble out into fresh air. We take in great, gulping breaths. I'm also blowing out big breaths because I feel like the stench has somehow coated my lungs. And my skin. And my clothes.

And as unpleasant as all this is, I'm feeling pretty accomplished. I totally managed not to throw up.

Greta is not so much golden as she is green.

Pinky sighs. "All right. We've got to get rid of this stench before I smash something. There's a premium boutique up ahead. I'll treat you both to a new outfit."

What's a premium boutique?

Inside, we're whisked away to private rooms where I'm thrown into a place that, on Earth, we'd call a day spa. I'm stripped, washed, steamed, exfoliated, dried, and wrapped in a soft, warm towel before I even know what's happening.

Literally a warm towel. Not like it's thick and keeps me warm, but this thing feels like it's been soaking up sun rays for the past few hours.

It's super nice.

I'm liking this premium boutique concept so far. All I smell now is a fresh laundry sort of scent combined with the faintest hint of carnations.

Two salespeople lead me out to a room that's entirely off-white, from the floor to the chairs to the walls. It's like a fancy snowstorm.

Before I really know what's happening, I'm sitting on the couch with my feet up. There's a glass of wine to my left, and I'm holding a bowl of tater tots.

Ah, it's you, tater tots. We meet again.

I'm wary of them, of course. The last time I had them, one of them tried to choke me to death. But darn if they don't smell amazing. There's this aroma. It's potatoey, and there's the indescribable scent of something that's deep-fried. But it's even better than that. There's an aroma that I can only describe as what I firmly hope nirvana smells like. Or heaven. Or blingdockville. Or whatever afterlife one ascribes to.

I need to eat these tater tots. My stomach yowls like a cat that's been challenged to a fight.

I do a quick mental calculation of Greta's distance from me at this moment, and the likelihood of my choking to death if I'm being very, very careful.

My estimation is higher than I'd prefer it to be for an action-positive situation, but man, these tater tots smell so good that I throw caution to the wind and delicately pick one up and take a judicious nibble.

It's official. I'm a wild, risk-taking adventurer.

This is, hands-down, the best tater tot I've ever eaten. All the others I've had prior to now were nothing compared to this.

This Mebdarian premium boutique thing is working out for me. So far.

Four people walk in via single-file progression. They're all dressed similarly, in a pair of pants and shirt that's either a polo or a tee.

Is this going to be some kind of dance battle?

I feel like it's going to be some kind of dance battle.

I am so not equipped for this.

But contrary to my initial impression, these four turn out to be models. The two men and two women stand before me and take turns striking poses, showing off the wares.

I'm not sure how to react.

Sure, I know I wear a certain kind of clothing. It's a survival technique. But they're all pretty much wearing the same thing. How am I supposed to choose something? And does choosing one thing over another mean something bad for the one I don't choose?

I'm unaware of the context of my choices.

The minutes pass, the posing continues, and I feel an awkwardness setting in. I'm supposed to choose one of these outfits.

They're all basically the same thing, though, and I don't want to hurt the models' feelings. What if their job is somehow tied to how many outfits they successfully model?

I'm not prepared to end someone's livelihood with a random selection of boring apparel.

Just as I'm beginning to feel deeply uncomfortable, inspiration strikes me. Pinky-sized inspiration.

"Is it possible," I ask, trying to sound as if this is a completely normal request, "for a dance battle to determine the victor?"

Four models and two shopping assistants light up with the joy of national pride and a passion for sick beats and even sicker dance moves.

"Really?" The senior assistant seems to think my suggestion is too good to be true.

"Absolutely," I say decisively, as if I know what I'm getting myself into.

Just between you and me, I have *no* idea what I'm getting myself into.

The younger shopping assistant sweeps in dramatically. Somehow, this seems important to the ritual. "A challenge has been issued!" she declared grandly. "Do you accept?"

All four models agree with enthusiasm and the kind of belligerence that comes with someone trying to make an impression of toughness.

I wonder what's going on with Pinky's and Greta's shopping experiences.

"Let the battle begin!" the assistant announces.

Music starts a pulse-pounding beat that is genuinely hard to resist. These Mebdarians know their dance tunes.

The assistant dramatically leaves the display area in front of me, moving to rejoin the other assistant in the back.

By some manner of decision-making unknowable to me, the dance/model competitors select one person to begin.

It's the taller of the two men. He's rather good-looking, if you like the broad-shouldered Adonis type, and he begins some basic-looking sidestepping moves, but quickly moves on to a variety of flips, drops, and hip thrusting.

He's showboating, in my opinion. The flips are very acrobatic but don't really go along with the music. The hip thrusting might please the ladies, but it does absolutely nothing for me. Frankly, I'm not that impressed.

Then the shorter of the two women begins her bit. She's probably the youngest of the group, and while she's got some good moves, they're unrefined and lacking in true mastery.

Before you ask, I do feel like I'm a judge of true Mebdarian mastery of the dance. I've seen Pinky break it down pro-style. It's a high bar, and frankly, I doubt any of these clothing models can reach it.

The second woman struts out and, okay, she's got some skills. Now we're talking. She's doing spins and pliés and other stuff I don't have words for, but believe me, it's fancy. Then she busts out some breakdancing, and we're finally getting to the kind of variety I expected from a Mebdarian dance battle.

When she's done, she's definitely in the lead, as far as my vote goes. If I get a vote. I'm unclear on that as of yet. But the final guy comes out of his corner swinging, and I mean that literally. He's throwing some kind of dance-type punches and doing these jump spins that I can't really describe except to say that he launches his body so that it's horizontal to the floor, and he's somehow spinning. Then he's on his feet and doing all these level changes and quick, sharp movements, and the winner is clear in my mind.

I'm curious if the others see the competition differently. I mean, people think different things are good, and just because I think he's the best doesn't meant that the other people here do.

But the others duck their heads in submission and there's a tacit agreement. The winner raises his arms in victory and the rest of us applaud.

Fortunately, those who didn't win seem pleased for him rather than disgruntled that they've lost.

I think that's nice.

The older shopping assistant comes forward again. "Mr. Kenny, do you agree that this is your outfit?"

She gestures at the man who won the battle. He's wearing slacks that have a hint of olive green, but the shirt's white, so I still feel okay about it.

"Yes, I do. Thank you very much."

"Woohoo!" The winning dancer/model comes forward and shakes my hand vigorously. "Thanks, man. I never sold an outfit by dance battle before. That's awesome."

"My friend told me that they're popular here," I say. "You're quite good. I bet you win frequently."

"Almost always." His words are belied by his modest duck of the head and downcast eyes.

At least he's not all cocky about his skills.

"There's this one woman, though, that I've always wanted to battle. She's a legend. She tends to be off-planet a lot, though."

"That's a shame," I say. "But thank you for the outfit. I'm sure I'll enjoy it."

"Yeah you will!" he exclaims. "This is one hundred percent Mebdarian cotton. Lots of planets use cotton, but we Mebdarians invented it, you know."

"Um, right," I agree.

Apparently this "Mebdarians did it first" thing is not specific to Pinky. That's interesting.

I'm ushered to a dressing room and given my new outfit, which is identical to the one worn by the dancing king.

I have to admit that the fabric is soft and breathes really well. I feel a little daring in the pants, too, given their hint of greenish tint.

Just to be extra sure I have enough clothing for this trip, I order the runner-up's outfit, too. It's a cream-colored shirt with khaki pants that's right in my wheelhouse.

As the sales assistants are handing me my bags, Greta emerges wearing a cute pink sundress and a pair of sandals.

She sees me, smiles, and I want to frame the moment, because having her smile just to see me is the best thing that will ever happen to me in my entire life.

"You found something," she says. "I was worried they wouldn't have anything for you."

"What, like all their clothes for guys would be glittery or neon or something?"

She looks embarrassed but amused by her embarrassment. It's super cute. She edges closer to say in a whisper, "Well, you never know on a different planet. I try to know all the most prominent facts about planets that Chance Fleet visits, but I don't know a ton about Mebdar II."

"I think I did okay," I say. I'm about to tell her about the dance battle when Pinky emerges.

"Whoa." The word comes out of my mouth all on its own.

Pinky halts and looks down at herself. "That good? Huh. I don't even have my new top yet. They're altering it for me. Should be done in a few minutes."

Have we ever talked about Pinky's usual clothing style? She tends to wear hiphugger pants and a tank top that shows just a bit of her rock-hard abs and every bit of her bulging biceps.

Right now, she's wearing a pair of blue pants in her typical style, but only a sports bra. This gives me the entire view of her abs, which look like a spaceship could crash into them and be dashed into space dust.

Greta leaps to my aid. "Those pants are great on you! They really show off your figure."

I nod. It's my only defense.

Pinky nods with understanding. "Ah, I gotcha. Yeah. These pants were just waiting for someone to come along and make them work. And here I am."

Have I ever mentioned how much I admire her confidence? I wish I had just a speck of that.

An assistant comes in and delivers the halter top. "Here we are. Do you want to go to a changing room to try it on?"

"No," Pinky says, in her blunt way. "Why?"

"Oh." The girl blinks. "No reason."

She hands over the top and backs away slowly.

Pinky pulls it over her head and smooths it into place. "What do you two think? Is it too blue? I don't wear much blue."

"No, you look great," I assure her. 'You looked great before, too. But now, I'd estimate you look ten percent even greater."

She points a finger at me and makes a clicking sound. I know from experience that this is a good thing, so I'm not alarmed. "It's the pants," she says decisively.

"I think you're right," Greta agrees.

After a long look in a long mirror, Pinky decides she approves of the outfit. She takes a step back and snaps into her favorite pose, with one hip thrust out and one finger up in the air.

Behind me, I hear a gasp.

I turn and see the winning dancer/model whose outfit I purchased.

He only has eyes for Pinky. "It's her!"

Oh, crap. Did Pinky visit the store before and rip something off the wall or something? But the dude doesn't look outraged—he looks awed.

I put it all together. He said there was a dancing legend he hoped to meet, who was rarely on the planet.

And here she is.

"Uh, I think this is a fan of yours, Pinky," I say, indicating the guy.

"Oh yeah?" She looks over her shoulder. "Always glad to meet a fan."

She comes over and stares at the guy with an eyebrow raised.

I elbow him. He looks at me, puzzled.

It's a rare occasion that I have the answer to anything, but I lean in and quietly say, "Tell her how much you like her."

"Oh! Right!" He straightens. "I've seen videos of you on the lightstream. You're amazing. I've always hoped to meet you in person."

"That's very brave of you," Pinky says.

There's an awkward pause.

I poke the guy. Flattery is always a good plan.

"Ow. I mean, wow!" he exclaims. "My friends will be so jealous."

This seems to please Pinky. "You want an autograph?"

"Sure!" he agrees.

Pinky says, "Well, go grab a marker or something, kid."

He comes back with a black felt-tip marker and a shopping bag. "I couldn't find any paper. This is all I could think of."

He indicates the bag sheepishly.

"I don't sign trash, dude." Nonetheless, Pinky takes the marker from him.

For a moment, I wonder what she'll do with it, then she leans in and signs her name with a flourish right on his forehead. She dots the "I" with a little heart.

Funny. I wouldn't have thought Pinky was a heart dotter.

"There ya go!" she says. "Now you can prove it to your friends."

She hands him the marker and turns to leave. "We're outta here. Dance well, store associate."

"Uh," the guy says, wearing her signature on his forehead. "I will. Thanks."

I wonder if this kind of thing is normal for Pinky. He did say she was a legend. She doesn't seem to let it go to her head, though. She looks as steely and focused as ever.

We pay our bills and roll out into the streets of...somewhere on Mebdar II looking like a million credits and not knowing what will happen next.

8

As we strut down the main avenue of the shopping district of Pinky's hometown of Patzer, I get my first good look at the place. Previously, I was too overwhelmed by the noxious stench to really notice my surroundings.

It's nice. It reminds me of where I'm from, actually. Patzer is a lot like New France/Old New York, except cleaner and more sparkly.

Literally. These people like their glitz. The trash cans are glittery and storefronts have that shiny/wet plastic look that's so popular these days.

A voice calls out, "Get your fried dough here."

Pinky veers off course, to the source. Greta and I follow in her wake.

"What ya got?" Pinky asks.

"Best fried dough in Patzer," the man assures her.

"Cinnamon sugar or powdered sugar?" she asks. "My friend here doesn't do well with powdered." She indicates me with a tilt of her head. Pinky can be really thoughtful like that sometimes.

She's right. No matter how hard I try, I always inhale at the wrong time and suck the stuff right into my lungs.

“Your choice!” the man declares jovially.

“Cool.” Pinky nods. “I’ll take all of it.”

“All of...what?” he asks, suddenly uncertain.

“What were you just offering?” she stares at him as if his ass has suddenly fallen off, and is just lying there on the ground behind him.

“Uh...you want *all* of the fried dough I have?” He squints a little as he says it, as if worried that this is the wrong response.

I like a lot of things about Pinky, but her ability to make people deeply, deeply uncomfortable over nothing at all is one of my favorites. So long as that power isn’t directed at me, of course.

“What are we not clear on, here?” Pinky asks.

The man snaps into action, straightening his apron and opening the door to his dough machine. “Nothing at all, ma’am. All the dough. Right away.”

“Good,” Pinky says, “but don’t call me ma’am.”

The fried dough purveyor freezes, a wary expression coming over his face.

“Don’t even think about calling me sir,” she warns.

He probably wishes he’d never called out “fried dough” at us.

“The customer’s always right,” he says resolutely, pulling out scoop after scoop of balls of fried dough.

Once he has them all in a large box, he grabs a large ladle and begins cascading cinnamon sugar over the dough with exceptional flair. His arm extends all the way as he plunges the ladle into a bucket of sugar and cinnamon, then whips it out, does a little twirl, and makes a big flashy show of sprinkling the sugar into the box.

Ladle after ladle of sugar goes into the box, and I begin to think about diabetes.

Then with quick movements, he closes up the box, and gives it a shake. But not just any shake. He shakes it while spinning around and doing a shoulder shimmy.

He turns the box over, bends at the waist, and presents it

to Pinky.

I should have expected such a move, but I did not.

She transfers the credits for the dough, holding the box under her arm.

"Nice. Dance well, dude." She gives him a thumbs-up.

He smiles and salutes her. "You too!"

"Oh, I always dance well. The best." She winks at him, then resumes strutting down the street.

Greta and I hurry after her.

"Is that how you say goodbye here?" Greta asks. "The dance well thing?"

"It's more like, 'see you later' than goodbye. More casual." Pinky opens the box and pops a ball of fried dough into her mouth. "Yeah, that's good."

She passes one to Greta, then one to me. I carefully bite into it.

"This is delicious." I take another bite. The dough is crispy on the outside, but soft and heavenly inside.

It's amazing.

"Of course it is." She inhales a half-dozen of them, one right after the other. "It's nice to be home."

She leads us to a bus stop where we sit on a bench and eat fried dough.

Apparently, when on Medbar II, one rides the bus.

"How far is your brother's house from here?" Greta asks.

"Twenty minutes by bus. Ten minutes if we walked it." Pinky tosses another dough ball into her mouth and offers me another.

Still thinking of diabetes, I shake my head and do a "no thanks" kind of smile.

"So why don't we just walk?" Greta asks.

"And miss the bus?" Pinky asks incredulously.

I am now both excited and nervous about this bus ride.

But mostly nervous.

When the bus pulls around the corner, I am awed, amazed,

and confused. It's shaped like an aerodynamic chicken, with the head facing forward as the bus moves down the road. Its beak appears to be open in a warrior scream, and this provides the opening for the windshield. Armor is painted on in gleaming bronze.

I say words I never expected to say. "Why is the bus a chicken?"

Pinky crushes the now-empty box between her hands. "Because my brother lives on the chicken line. Duh."

Sigh.

This isn't just me being a sectarian rube. This is weird. Greta looks just as puzzled as I feel.

I don't want to get on the warrior chicken bus. I don't. There's no telling what this experience is going to be, and everything in my body rebels against it.

I'm about to suggest we walk, but Pinky's already stepping toward the bus and Greta moves next to me and puts her hand in mine.

She smiles into my eyes and I feel stronger. For her, I will ride the warrior chicken bus.

I love her so much.

With my other hand, I squeeze the green luck stone she gave me.

Kenogu.

We get on the bus.

Pinky goes first, stepping up the three stairs and moving in. I go ahead of Greta, still holding her hand.

Then Pinky goes up more stairs.

Wait, what?

This is a double-decker bus. I guess I'd been too distracted by the rebel yell of the warrior chicken to notice that bit.

Sighing, I trudge up the steps.

Heights are not good for my people. Neither is any mode of transit. Now I'm combining them. Yay.

That's a sarcastic "yay." I am not actually jubilant about this.

When we arrive on the top level of the bus, everything looks surprisingly normal. Not unlike something you'd see on a sight-seeing tour of New France. Less crowded, though. There are only a dozen people up here, though there are accommodations for four times as many people.

Greta sits down first, leaving me an aisle seat, while Pinky takes the pair of seats behind us.

I wait for something to happen.

The bus smoothly takes off and proceeds at an entirely reasonable rate of speed.

The woman in front of me turns around and asks, "Excuse me, do you have the time?"

I do have a chronometer in my pocket, but I haven't adjusted it for local time. "Sorry, I'm not from around here."

She squints at me. "Do they not have time where you're from?"

"They do," I assure her. "It's just different there."

Her eyes go round and she leans in and whispers, "Are you a time traveler? I won't tell."

As far as I know, backward time travel simply isn't possible, due to the fact that it would break the second law of thermodynamics. And thus far, no one has figured out forward time travel. So does she think I'm from the past or from the future?

I feel like I need more details to properly answer her question.

"You mean, like from the past or from the future?" I ask. "Or someone who just shifts back and forth?"

"Are you any of those?" she asks, turning around more fully, looking extremely interested.

"No. But I was curious where you thought I might have come from. If I came from the past, I wouldn't be able to get back there. So if I were a time traveler, and had the ability to do it more than once, I could move forward again, but never backward. So, you see, if you were hoping I could go back into the past and fix something for you, that just wouldn't be possible. If I were a time traveler. Which I'm not."

She looks at me for a full ten seconds. "You are, aren't you? You're just saying you aren't because you have to, right?"

"Yes," I agree. "Because it's not true."

"Right." She nods knowingly. "Gotcha." She winks and turns back around to face forward.

"I handled that poorly, didn't I?" I ask Greta in a low voice.

"You could have done a lot better," she admits. "But think of it this way—she got to meet a time traveler. So it's a good day for her."

I smile. It's a good point.

She grins at me and gives my arm a squeeze. "You make even a simple bus ride fun."

"Yeah?" I wiggle my eyebrows at her. "I could do more, but I don't know if you can handle all this." I gesture at myself.

She bursts into laughter and gives me a sideways hug and a straightways smooch.

Nice. Other than my mishandling of the time traveler question, so far we're doing okay. There's a light breeze caused by the moderate speed of the bus, and the view is actually quite enjoyable. I have a good view of Patzer.

It's downright pleasant, and that's not just because I'm riding the wave of making Greta laugh and get affectionate.

Twenty minutes after we boarded, Pinky stands. "This is our stop."

I'm puzzled. I expected more. "But nothing's happened."

"What do you mean?" she asks. "We arrived at our destination, didn't we? Isn't that the point of the bus?"

I carefully follow her down to the bus steps. When we're on the street and the bus is driving away, I pick up the conversation. "You were so adamant about the bus. I thought riding it would be more..." I try to come up with the right word.

"Eventful," Greta finishes.

I shoot her a grateful look. I lost her hand on the way off the bus, when I clutched the handrails like a cat trying to avoid a bath. I'm not overly bothered by this, though, as I plan to hold her hand again in the not-too-distant future.

"Oh." Pinky shrugs. "No, the bus rides aren't anything special. But if you pass by the Barclay apartments at this time of day, there's a good chance that the guy in 701D will be naked."

I'm pretty sure there's nothing I could say that wouldn't come out very poorly, so I opt for my trusty standby of remaining silent.

Greta is more intrepid. "Why does he do this, and how do you know about it?"

"Oh, we dated a long time ago. Only a so-so dancer, but he sure looks great naked. He gets home this time of day and takes a shower, then walks around his apartment to air dry."

Greta and I exchange a look. A guy Pinky once dated? I have to see this guy.

Not, like, while he's air-drying. Don't get the wrong idea. But any guy who can get Pinky's attention in that way must be something really special. At least, to her way of thinking.

I can tell Greta's thinking the same thing.

At least, I hope she is. It'd be a real kick in the pants to find out later that her look of interest is because she wants to get an eyeful of him during his drying-off time.

Pinky's a fast walker, so Greta and I have to hurry to keep up with her. Eight blocks later, we arrive at her brother's place.

What will he be like, this brother of Pinky's? She's never mentioned whether there are other mutants in her family or not. She's never talked much about her family before her brother's request to find him a wife.

I have no idea what to expect.

Pinky rings a bell and we stand at the door, waiting.

At least this bit is familiar.

The door opens and a good-looking, non-mutant man blinks

in surprise when he sees us standing there. "Pinky! Wow. That was quick."

Pinky shrugs. "I like to get things crossed off the to-do list."

He gestures us in and closes the door behind us. Then he gives Pinky a quick hug. "It's great to see you."

"Nice to see you, too, Jon, even though you're putting me to work." She returns his hug with one arm, patting him on the back and then setting him aside.

Pinky's not much of a hugger.

I study her brother. I can see a resemblance around the eyes and nose, I think. He's very good-looking, with a nice muscular build. For a non-mutant. I'd guess he's about my age, and he has a pleasant smile.

He shakes my hand perfunctorily, his gaze skating over me so he can move on to Greta.

You know that feeling you get in the pit of your stomach when things start to go sideways on you? I'm getting that feeling.

Jon takes Greta's hands gently in his and smiles down into her eyes. "I'm so glad to meet you."

"It's nice to meet you, too." Greta glows with the luminescence she has when she's happy. Which is almost always. "I'm so pleased to meet a member of Pinky's family. She's one of my very best friends."

"That's great!" Jon beams. "In-laws should get along."

I knew it. He thinks Greta is his new girlfriend.

Pinky puts a heavy hand on her brother's shoulder. "As fun as it is to watch Charlie squirm, I have to disappoint you, bro. Greta isn't for you."

He's still holding her hands. Disappointment creases his face. "She's not?"

Pinky shakes her head firmly. "Nope."

He peers at Greta hopefully. "But maybe she could be?"

He's conveniently failed to take note of Pinky's reference to me, and the fact that I don't like this situation, so he surely hasn't taken the time to reason out just why that might be.

It's like I'm not even here. Typical.

"I don't think so," Pinky says.

Greta's glow has increased slightly. I think she's blushing. She edges closer to me and pulls her hands out of his grip, placing them on my arm instead.

Her touch seems to make Jon aware of me. He looks from her to me with a faint look of puzzlement.

He extends his hand. "Nice to meet you, I'm Jon Peach."

Dammit. This is just insulting.

"Yeah," I say, "we met a minute ago. But wait a minute..."

I look from Jon to Pinky. "Your name is Peach?"

Pinky looks at me like I'm an idiot. "Am I not always saying that I'm a Peach?"

Yes. Yes, she is. "I thought it was a phrase."

Apparently, Greta did too, because she ventures, "So your name is Pinky Peach? That's so cute."

"Yeah, great name, right?" Pinky looks proud.

"Terrific name!" Greta agrees.

Still disgruntled by Jon's misunderstanding about Greta, I only nod.

It is a great name, though.

"Right," Jon says. "So...when am I meeting the girl you've chosen for me?"

"Soon," Pinky assured him. "As soon as I find her."

He sighs. "You haven't started looking?"

She gives him a severe look. "I've always been looking. I just haven't found the right girl yet. Not just anyone is good enough for a Peach."

He appears to be mollified. "All right. Well...can I get you all some tea or a fizzy cola?"

Carbonation is unpredictable sometimes, and I tend to avoid it. I opt for tea, while Greta and Pinky agree to cola.

We sit down at the four-person table near the kitchen and while Pinky and Jon catch up with each other, I get a chance to look around without being too obvious about it.

It's roomy enough, and the furnishings look comfortable and well-made. He seems to like shades of yellow and green, which makes me think he's either into nature or just likes cheerful colors.

Greta speaks up, which brings me back to the conversation, which had become a bunch of references to people I don't know.

She says, "So you're a doctor?"

Jon nods. "Pediatric surgeon."

"He just became head of the department," Pinky adds proudly.

Great. That's just great. Not only is he good-looking and related to Pinky, but he's also smart, successful, and likes kids.

Meanwhile, I'm afraid of forks.

Sigh.

On the bright side, surely tons of eligible women would be interested in this guy. It shouldn't be too hard to find someone for him.

I hope that will happen very soon.

For his sake, you know. Not mine. He seems lonely.

That's sad.

"So what do you do, Kenny?" Jon asks me.

"It's Charlie, actually," I say. "Kenny is my last name."

"Right. Sorry." Jon looks chagrined.

"I did the same thing when I first met him," Greta says.

Oh, good. They have things in common now.

"I'm a statistician," I say. "I work remotely while cruising the universe on the *Second Chance*."

That sounds cool, right? I really want to sound cool at this particular moment.

"That sounds great," Jon says. "I'm sure you have a lot of adventures that way."

"We do!" Greta says enthusiastically. "Charlie's the best. Since he came aboard, we've been chased by loan sharks, attacked by blagrooks, and we even battled the cyborg union—and won."

"Wow." Jon seems impressed. "How did you get on the wrong side of loan sharks? Did you end up short on money?"

"Not me," I say quickly.

"It was his wife," Pinky says, ever helpful.

"Ex-wife," Greta corrects.

"You were married?" Jon looks at me like he's seeing for the first time. Since, you know, five minutes ago, when he realized I'd been standing in his home.

"Not on purpose. It was an Albacore wedding. Unfortunate misunderstanding," I explain.

"Ah." He nods. "Had that happen to a friend once. Never saw him again."

"That's a shame," I say.

"He sleeps with the fishes now." Jon shakes his head sadly.

Damn, that sucks. I didn't expect this conversation to take such a tragic turn.

"With his wife, I mean," Jon says. "He decided to go with it and see how it went."

I laugh. I have to admit, after my brief relationship with Oollooleeloo, I've become quite fond of fish puns.

It probably means I'm a terrible person.

"Speaking of seafood, have you guys eaten?" Jon asks. "We could go for dinner. My treat."

Pinky stands. "That's all I need to hear."

Greta nods. "That sounds great. You can introduce us to the local cuisine."

She's so cute. She's always interested in learning about other people.

They look at me, and I'm stuck.

"Sure," I agree gamely.

I hope Mebdarian food doesn't throw me any curve balls.

9

WE END up in what I can only describe as a slick, fancy diner. All the surfaces are shiny and smooth, and the color scheme is decidedly neon. The food and the service, though, are far from casual dining.

These people take their diners seriously.

A woman in a tuxedo-like outfit approaches with a towel over her arm and offers us a wine menu.

She seems unaware that her otherwise formal outfit is glittering and sparkling like diamonds or a show dancer's costume.

Or maybe I have it wrong. Maybe on Mebdar II, glitter and sparkles are the epitome of refinement.

I have some things to think about. Maybe later I'll ask Pinky about it, if my constitution is feeling strong enough for whatever dents Pinky will put in it as she answers.

Which means I probably won't ask. But maybe Greta will.

For a redshirt, ordering food is always a delicate process. There are certain foods where choking hazards are to be expected. Olives, for example. It's entirely possible for one to have a pit inside. Even if I don't choke on it, I'll probably break a tooth on it. Nope. No whole olives for me.

Fish is likewise out if it might have bones still inside. And since this is me we're talking about, it would be full of them. I once found a bone in an avocado. I never did come up with a reasonable explanation for that.

I decide on the potato soup. According to the description, baby potatoes have been harvested at the peak of youthful perfection, slow-roasted, and joined by a medley of leeks, onions, and the essence of smoke.

I don't know what smoke essence is, as it would seem to me that smoke is smoke, and the mere essence would be, what...the smell?

Additionally, I feel a little bad about those baby potatoes. I mean, how sad to be cut down in their youth. On the other hand, they're spoken of in such hallowed tones that I feel like these potatoes have probably had a much better life than I have.

Pinky and Jon opt for steak and grilled cheese, which is apparently a thing here.

Greta chooses tomato bisque and something called "Dunsquack's Rotiliodromomede."

Neither of us knows what that means, and she's ordered it just to see what happens.

Pinky looks impressed when Greta orders it. "That's not one that offworlders usually tackle."

I wish, just once, I could impress Pinky.

"It sounds interesting," Greta says. "I like to try new things."

"And I like that about you," Pinky says.

Jon looks like he's going to tell Greta that he likes that about her, too, so I jab my finger in a random direction and say, "What's that about?"

It's a safe move. Nearly everything here requires explanation. It's not that things are so entirely foreign, on the whole. It's just that they're presented in an unexpected manner.

Pinky's gaze follows the direction of my point. "It's a sign indicating the direction of the restrooms."

I, too, follow the direction of my point, and see that I've indicated a very basic, very obvious sign.

Yeah, that's about my luck.

Not wanting to seem entirely lame in front of Greta, I say, "No, not that. The purple thing to the left."

There's a swirled glass thing with some symbols I don't recognize.

Pinky looks again. "Oh. That just indicates that dance battles aren't to take place in the dining room, and should be taken in that direction."

"Really?" Even with the Mebdarian fondness for dance battles, the idea of people pausing a meal to throw down seems odd.

"Of course." Pinky looks at me, puzzled. "You think people should have dance battles right here, putting their feet in your soup and landing on your table? I've been to that club, and it's fine for when you're young, but I'm too old for that shit."

"Ah," I say. "That's a good point. I'm sure you're right."

"Of course I am," Pinky retorts. "I'm a Peach."

Jon grins and holds up his water glass so she can bump it with hers.

Apparently that's a thing in their family. I try to imagine something similar among the Kenny clan.

Of course my grandmother fell into a chipper-shredder in the middle of a department store, one of my relatives might say. *I'm a Kenny.* Then we all bump fists.

I don't care for this particular mental image. It's for the best that we never engage in such one-upmanship.

We engage in small talk until the food arrives.

Hm. My soup has arrived with an unadvertised breadstick. I pick up the baked good, turn it over, then break it in half to inspect it for dubious content.

It's just a breadstick. So that's cool. I like breadsticks.

My soup is tasty. My breadstick is good. I'm in good shape this evening.

Greta, on the other hand, struggles with her Dunsquack's Rotiliodromomede. As it turns out, it's an artichoke, stuffed inside some kind of poultry, stuffed inside a pumpkin. It's huge and takes up half the table. Greta's still working on not obliterating her food into crumbs before eating it, so she's reasonably intimidated by this behemoth.

Fortunately our friend, the behemoth, helps her out. "Want to share that, Greta? I'm always up for a Dunsquack's Rotiliodromomede."

Yeah, that's right. Pinky can be both subtle and merciful.

"Absolutely," Greta agrees, grateful. "I didn't realize it would be so big."

The rest of the meal passes pleasantly enough. I don't choke on my soup and Jon and Pinky do a respectable job of helping Greta with the thing she ordered. She says it's quite tasty, but I stick with my soup.

After dinner, we walk down the main avenue together. Somehow, Jon manages to get next to Greta, which leaves me walking behind them with Pinky.

I'm less than thrilled with this arrangement.

"So," I say, a little more loudly than I need to. "We're going to start looking around for Jon's wife tomorrow, right?"

"Definitely," Pinky agrees. "I'm going to take a look through the matchmaking database and see if I can compile a list of likely women for us to meet with."

I had said "we" as a morale-boosting kind of thing, but it appears that I'm actually going to be involved with this process. And apparently it involves a matchmaking service, in spite of Pinky's previous negativity toward dating profiles. They must be different things.

"That sounds promising," I say.

"We'll see." Pinky sounds cynical. "The database doesn't tend to have the best ones, because they're usually matched up by people they know personally. But sometimes, a person can get lucky."

"What about asking people you know, then?" I ask, sure I'm saying something dumb. "Network among the people you have some familiarity with."

Rather than deal me a crushing blow, Pinky purses her lips. "It's a good idea. I'll put the word out."

Wow. Was I actually helpful just now? I feel really good about that. And not just because it means getting Jon's attention off of Greta.

Though that's a really good side benefit.

"Are you sure you three don't want to stay with me at my place?" Jon asks. "I could pull out cots."

"No way," Pinky declares. "Between Charlie's luck and Greta's excessive good cheer, I'd end up murdering someone. Plus, you all sleep. Like, for hours. Am I supposed to tiptoe around during that?"

"Right," Jon says. "Okay. I'm scheduled to work tomorrow, though. Should I call off?"

"No." Pinky frowns at him. "I'll call you when I've found a good one."

"Find more than one," he jokes. "Then I can choose among them."

"Don't make me break you." She says it in a flippant way, but I feel like she means it.

Jon just smiles, though, and turns down a side street back toward his apartment. "I'll hope to hear from you soon, then. Don't keep me waiting."

"Dance well," Pinky calls after him, ignoring his words.

"So where are we staying?" Greta asks as we continue walking.

The sky has grown dark, but bright lights keep the main avenue illuminated. Overall, there's a party sort of atmosphere. The kind of charged energy where you feel like anything could happen at any time.

Naturally, I don't care for it. There's just too much statistical variability.

"I made us reservations at a local bed and breakfast. Nice place. I thought about a hotel, but figured a B&B would give you more of the authentic Mebdar II experience. Plus, it's cheaper, and has better food."

"Sounds great," Greta enthuses.

"They have three rooms, and I nabbed all of them," Pinky continues. "I'll get the suite, naturally, since I need more space. Greta, you get the blue room, and Charlie, you get the brown room. I already had our bags routed there, so they should be waiting for us by the time we get there."

The brown room might not sound auspicious to you, but since brown is just a darker shade of beige, I'm moderately encouraged.

Plus, I'm tired and inclined not to be too picky.

A few minutes later we arrive at the B&B where we're greeted by an enthusiastic man and woman who usher us to our rooms, show us the amenities, and deliver warm oatmeal raisin cookies to us while we're settling in.

Alone in my room with my cookies, I relax. Everything's some shade of brown, tan, or off-white, and it's all really boring. It's perfect. I lay down on the plush, comfortable bed and bite into a cookie.

It's delicious. No doubt if I asked, I'd be assured that Mebdarians invented oatmeal raisin cookies. Or maybe all cookies.

Regardless of where the progenitors originated, these cookies are fantastic.

They remind me of my nana. Not because they taste the same,

but because they couldn't be more different than what Nana makes.

I hope she's doing well up there on the *Second Chance*, and not getting busted for illegal gambling in interstellar space.

10

I'm not the kind of person who sleeps well in unfamiliar surroundings, but I sleep wonderfully at the bed and breakfast. Maybe it's the bland color scheme of the room or the white noise machine by the bed that I've set to an electronic hum, but I wake up feeling great.

Breakfast is excellent, too. When I join the others in the dining room, we're served eggs benedict, beans and toast, and the most delicious cheese-filled muffins.

Naturally, with all this good fortune coming my way, I'm waiting for things to shift the other way.

After breakfast, Greta and I tag along with Pinky to the matchmaking headquarters. We have nothing better to do, and frankly, I'm curious to see such a place.

As it turns out, the reality does not live up to my expectations.

The matchmaking headquarters of this part of the planet is right here in Patzer. I expected gleaming surfaces and shiny things, but it's as dull as a corporate office building on Earth.

A really boring corporate office building. The kind with low-grade carpet and faux-wood veneer on the desks.

Naturally, I feel entirely at ease.

We approach a receptionist. Well, Pinky approaches. Greta and I just kind of follow her.

"Can I help you?" a young Mebdarian man asks.

"I need to find my brother a wife," Pinky says.

"Ahh, so is this your first visit here?" he asks.

"Yeah. I only have one brother."

"Okay. I assume you've never met with a matchmaking consultant, then."

"You assume correctly." Pinky eyes him.

"You're in luck," he says. "Our very best one is in today. If Sloan can't find your brother the perfect woman, then she doesn't exist."

"That's not the kind of negativity I'm looking for here, little buddy." Pinky leans down slightly, her attention fixed.

I've been on the other side of that stare. It's not nice.

"Uh, no, I didn't mean it as negative," the man says. "I meant it as positive. Sloan's the best. I'll go get her now!"

He leaps up and scurries away.

Two minutes later, a pretty, dark-haired woman approaches and extends her hand toward Pinky. "Hi, I'm Sloan Vanst. I understand you're looking to match your brother with someone special."

Pinky looks at the proffered hand. "You can put that away."

She said something similar soon after I first met her. It's a nice memory. I feel nostalgic.

Pinky continues, "And it depends on what you mean by 'special.' If you mean someone who stands out from others in a positive and likeable way, then yes. If you mean someone who stuffs tater tots up her nose, then no."

Sloan drops her hand to her side and smiles bravely. "Yes, I meant someone well suited to your brother. Likeable."

"Great," Pinky says. "How do we start?"

Sloan's overabundant smile eases. She clearly feels more confident now. "We'll have a meeting to discuss your brother, what kind of person he's looking for, and what you think would best suit him. Then there will be some questionnaires about habits and preferences."

"Everyone lies on those," Pinky says. "What's the point?"

Sloan nods, as if she anticipated this question. "People tend to misrepresent things in the same way, so we normalize to get a better picture."

"All right," Pinky agrees. "Let's go."

Sloan blinks. "Oh. Usually we set up an appointment."

"I'm on layover," Pinky says. "I only have a few days. Might as well get right to work, don't you think?"

"A few days?" Sloan asks. "I don't know if that will be enough time to..." she trails off, then straightens. "We'll do our best! I do have some time right now. I can always get lunch later. Right this way, please."

Sloan's office is more of the same banal, uninspired design as the rest of the building. The chairs look comfy, though.

"So are you two family members as well?" Sloan smiles at Greta and me.

"Oh, no," Greta says. "At least, not by blood. But Pinky's a friend so close that we consider her family. Charlie and I actually only met Jon last night. We probably won't be much help, but we're curious about this process, since it's different than how people get married on our planets."

Sloan chuckles. "Well, not all people here do it the traditional way, either. There are a lot of progressive people who choose their own spouses. And in some traditional families, a person can only do that once they've made a sincere effort at being set up."

"Are you married?" Greta asks.

"Me?" Sloan seems surprised by the question. "No, not yet. Someday."

Now I'm curious, too. "Have you tried having someone set you up?"

Sloan shakes her head. "I don't have any sisters, and no one has really tried. Doing it the traditional way would be nice, but I'll just have to wait until I meet someone on my own."

"What is it you like about the traditional method?" Greta asks.

Sloan glances at Pinky. "I don't mind answering, but is it okay with you? This isn't exactly why you came."

Pinky shrugs. "They like to ask questions. It's fine."

"Okay," Sloan says. "Well, I like the idea of being far less likely to divorce. That's a hard thing to go through. And matchmaking ensures that people get along well with their prospective in-laws. I don't know how it is where you're from, but here, if in-laws don't get along, it can be really awful for everyone involved." She taps her finger against her lips thoughtfully. "Plus, I think traditional things are nice, if they're still relevant. For a lot of people, coming here is an exciting rite of passage."

"Like getting a driver's license or graduating school?" Greta asks.

"Exactly." Sloan nods. "So, let's talk about Jon."

"He's a doctor," Pinky says. "He cares about people. He's successful and good-looking, and has a decent sense of humor. He's not as good as me at dance battles, but nobody is. He makes a good dance partner, though."

Sloan's making notes on a pad with her stylus. "I see. What kind of woman do you think would best suit him?"

"Well," Pinky says, "she shouldn't be petty or jealous. He hates that stuff. Someone with good self-confidence and intellect. Someone who won't get upset when he has to work extra hours. Someone who has her own job, so she isn't too dependent, but that job should have regular hours or they might have trouble finding time together."

Sloan nods, looking down at the pad. "Good. What five adjectives would you use to describe him? Words you haven't already used."

"Hm." Pinky's brow furrows as she thinks. "Reliable. Thoughtful. Adaptable. Honest. Polydactyl."

I look at her, startled. "What? He's a cat with extra toes?"

Pinky furrows her brow. "Is that what that means? No, not that. I mean...personable."

"Great." Sloan looks up, ignoring the misused word entirely. "With traits like those, it shouldn't be hard to find women who would be interested."

"Yeah, that's not the problem," Pinky agrees. "I could punch a random woman in the head on the bus and she'd probably like him. The issue is finding someone who's good enough for him."

If Sloan's taken aback by Pinky's choice of words, she doesn't show it. Maybe that head-punching thing is a common phrase here.

"Okay," Sloan says. "This is a great start. I'll send you the forms I told you about, one set for you and one set for him, and we'll get some further details. When you send them back, please include some pictures of him."

"Naked or clothed?" Pinky asks.

"Oh." This time, Sloan does seem perturbed. "Clothed, definitely."

"Good." Pinky cracks her knuckles. "The naked thing would be awkward, with me being his sister."

"Of course." Sloan's wearing a professional, pasted-on smile. She stands and starts to offer her hand before pulling it back. "It was lovely meeting you, and I look forward to working with you to find Jon the right person for him."

"Are we done already?" Pinky asks. "I kind of expected this to take longer."

"The first meeting is fairly short," Sloan says. "We'll go into further detail after you return the questionnaires."

"I"ll have them back to you within a couple hours," Pinky says. "I want to keep this train moving. I like trains, you know. Rode on one on Earth. Didn't get to shovel coal, but they gave me a really bitchin' hat, you know? All stripey and stuff."

Sloan nods as if she understands completely. "That's fantastic.

We'll try to keep the wheels rolling down the track. Once I get the questionnaires back, I'll do a little cross-matching, and call you back this afternoon. We'll fast-track this match."

"Great." Pinky stands. "Nice meeting you. I think you're going to do well for us."

"I promise to give it my best."

I decide to give the local farewell a try, because when on Mebdar II, do as the Mebdarian Twoians do.

"Dance well," I say.

Sloan nods and waves.

I totally nailed that.

As we file out of her office, we pass the guy at the reception desk.

"How did it go?" he asks.

"So far so good," Pinky says.

He nods. "You got lucky. Sloan's our best matchmaker. She's been at it for five years, and in all that time, none of her couples have divorced. They all seem to be very happy."

"Nice. That's some good kenogu," Pinky says.

"Sure is. We'll see you soon. Take care, dance well." The guy waves.

As we leave, Greta says, "The best matchmaker. That's great. I can't wait to see the woman she chooses."

Neither can I.

"WHAT SHOULD we do while we wait?" Greta asks when we get outside. "Do you want to go visit Jon? It's been a while since you saw him, right? Charlie and I can find something to do if you two want some brother-sister bonding time."

"Maybe tomorrow," Pinky says. "He can't get off work on such short notice, but tomorrow's his regular day off, so we'll see him then."

"So what should we do today?" I ask.

"I was thinking we could go to my favorite ice cream shop before I send those forms to Sloan," Pinky says.

"That sounds fun!" Greta looks excited about the prospect of a frozen treat.

"Hang on," I say. I've been at this long enough to know that things that sound like one thing are often something else entirely. Laundromats that are dance clubs. Bars that are ice cream shops. What might an ice cream shop be? "What do they have at this place?"

"All the normal stuff," Pinky says. "Sundaes, cones, milk-shakes. But they have some unique things, too. And they have food, too. Fried dough, sandwiches, hush puppies, that kind of thing."

"That sounds pretty normal," I say. I have to admit, I'm surprised. I expected something wacky. I bet you did, too. "Let's give it a try."

"Should we take the bus?" Greta asks.

"It's a couple miles away, outside the city center, so that's probably a good idea," Pinky says. "Unless you two want to enjoy a stroll. It's a nice walk."

I look at Greta and she looks at me. I shrug. "Whatever sounds good to you."

Not only do I get to be cool by letting her choose, but I also get to rely on her kenogu. It's a win-win for me.

"Let's ride the bus. We can always walk afterward," she decides.

"Cool." Pinky gestures toward the bus stop, a block away. "We'll want to get on the flamingo line."

I find this cute, given Pinky's fondness for that particular bird. "Is the bus line part of why you like this particular ice cream shop so much?"

We reach the bus stop and sit down on the bench. Pinky

purses her lips thoughtfully. "I think you might be right. I never really thought about it. I just like what I like."

"And I like that about you," I say. "You're always true to yourself."

I find it quite inspiring.

"Of course I am. Who else would I be true to?" Pinky shrugs and turns her face up to the sun, closing her eyes.

Indeed.

The flamingo bus pulls around the corner into my view, and I should have been prepared for the sight of it, but I wasn't.

The sheer pinkness of the bus would be startling enough. I mean, you just don't see a color like that covering the entirety of something huge like a double-decker bus. But then there's the big flamingo face staring out, with its black eyes and its black-tipped beak.

Instead of being a warrior, though, as the chicken bus depicted, the flamingo appears to be a winky, Don Juan sort. If this flamingo weren't, in fact, a bus, I feel like he would be very popular with the ladies.

I feel a reluctant, fleeting sense of envy. I know it isn't logical, even as I'm feeling it, but I feel it all the same.

I wish I could be as popular with the ladies as this inanimate object would be, if it were real.

Sad. So sad.

"Let's go." Without looking to make sure Greta and I are following, Pinky legs it over to the bus and climbs up to the top.

There's room enough that we could sit in the safer, enclosed lower portion, but nope. We're going up to the top.

Once there, I don't feel better about it, even though we rode this way once before without incident. I console myself with the extremely low statistical rate of double-decker-bird-bus-related injuries.

"So tell us about this ice cream shop," Greta says once we're settled in and the bus has started moving.

"Not sure what more I can really tell you," Pinky says. "Good ice cream. Decent atmosphere. Even the clientele isn't too stupid. Five out of five, would definitely go again."

She speaks as though reciting a review.

"Well, what's it called?" Greta asks.

"Billy and Nanny's. Most people just call it Billy's for short."

"Kind of stinks for Nanny," I muse.

"I guess," Pinky says. "But we all have our problems."

We fall silent for a couple of minutes until Greta says, "Some of these things we're passing look interesting. Can you point out some sights for us?"

"Sure," Pinky agrees gamely. "That right there"—she points—"is a building. I'm guessing some kind of business is in there. And that one"—she points again—"is an apartment building. People live there."

"Oh," Greta says. "Great."

Is Pinky joking? I feel like she's probably joking. That's exactly the kind of thing she'd joke about, and she'd be straight-faced just like this, too, because that's how she rolls.

However, I'm not certain she's joking, and I don't want to chuckle if she isn't.

Greta seems as uncertain as I am, and we lapse into silence again.

No further sights are pointed out.

Twenty minutes later, we get off the bus and I get my first look at Billy and Nanny's ice cream shop.

Goats.

There are goats everywhere. On the sign. In the windows. A large goat statue has been put right in front of the place. Kids are taking turns climbing on and sitting while their parents take pictures of them.

Right. Billy and Nanny. Goats.

"Does this place, by any chance," I ask, "specialize in goat milk ice cream?"

"Of course," Pinky says. "It's the best kind. I mean, other milks are good, too, but they just aren't as..." She frowns. "What's the word I'm looking for?"

"Goaty?" I offer helpfully.

"Yeah. Exactly. Goaty." Pinky nods and reaches for the door.

Beside me, Greta has gone silent and seems a bit stiff.

"Something wrong?" I ask her.

"Not exactly," she says uneasily. "This just reminds me of college."

Oh. Right. "The goat infestation."

"Yeah. They're cute and all, but they tend to ram into things with their heads. I guess I'm having a bit of a flashback."

"I don't think there are any real ones here," I say. "At least, I don't see any. And you can always hide behind Pinky. It's what I do."

That last bit slips out before I can grab it back, but you know what, it's done now.

She grins at me and squeezes my bicep, though, so I guess she liked it.

We hurry to follow Pinky, then realize we didn't hurry fast enough. Pinky's nowhere to be seen. Her passion for ice cream has apparently overridden her willingness to wait for us.

We step in on our own with a dawning feeling of amazement. This ice cream shop is big. Huge. Definitely much larger on the inside.

We're in some front atrium, and from here, I see signs to different areas. One says, "Goat Palace" and I'm pretty sure Greta and I are not going to head in that direction. The next one, at about ten o'clock from my position, says "Sprinkles and Jimmies." That sounds fun, and I like it, but I have to wonder, is there a difference between sprinkles and jimmies? I always thought they were the same thing. Are they in fact two distinct things, or is this sign just redundant?

At the noon position is a room labeled, "Confectionary." That, at least, seems straightforward. The two o'clock and four o'clock directions have rooms that are labeled "Grunt Work" and "Forget It," respectively.

"Which one do you think?" I ask Greta because her luck is bound to take us either where we ultimately want to go or someplace that will end up great anyway.

"Why don't you pick?" she suggests.

Apparently, she's in the mood for an adventure.

"Pinky's no doubt wondering where we are," I point out.

"Pinky's probably eating an octuple-scoop cone with extra everything right now. I figure we have some time on our hands," she says.

That sounds about right, actually.

"I feel like 'confection' is most likely to be correct, but I'm curious about the sprinkles versus jimmies thing," I say.

"I wondered about that too! Aren't they the same thing?"

"I thought so."

She tugs at my arm. "Let's go find out."

"Are you sure you don't want to go to the confectionary? I bet that's where the ice cream is." Admittedly, I'm feeling a bit less adventurous than she is.

"We'll do that next."

And we're off.

THE FIRST THING I notice about "Jimmies and Sprinkles," is that the way into it is a giant chute. A slide, I suppose, with an overhead machine dropping a never ending stream of soft, brightly colored balls as people sit down and slide to whatever awaits them below.

"I don't know about this," I say.

"It looks fun," Greta says, because of course she thinks it looks fun. "Let's try it."

I hesitate and she stands on her tiptoes and kisses me on the cheek. "Please?

Dammit.

"Okay," I agree.

This will be fine. Of course it will. It's just a slide. And Greta's right here, counterbalancing whatever my own luck might try to brew up.

We sit. I take a breath.

We slide.

And slide.

And slide.

Holy bejeezus, this is a long slide.

It's not an altogether terrible ride, and might even be a little bit fun once we stop.

Finally, we get to the end, which is, as I suspected, a giant ball pit.

You saw that coming too, right? Figuratively speaking?

As I swim my way through all the balls, I pray I don't touch anything wet. That's really all I want right now.

Success! I climb out and realize I've made it out before Greta. I reach down and help her get out, and feel quite manly about it.

"That was fun!" she exclaims. "I wonder what's next?"

Looking ahead, I see people standing in a line. Since the existence of a line generally means that people are supposed to stand in it, that's what we do. Every minute or two, we move forward a couple of steps, as per line-standing protocol.

"Oh," Greta says. "I see. This is where they make the sprinkles, or jimmies, or whatever. This is the factory part, so we can see them being made."

"Cool," I say. I'm not just playing it cool. I actually like seeing how things are made. Considering the dangers posed by industrial equipment, though, I've always done so at a distance via the lightstream.

But we move forward and I see massive amounts of sugar and

other things being poured into gigantic mixers. I'm a little surprised to see workers do a brief dance routine before activating the mixers, but not *too* surprised.

After the stuff is mixed, it forms a brightly colored crumbly kind of mixture. We've happened along at the right time to see pink and orange ones being made. The crumbly stuff gets dumped out of the mixers onto huge conveyers that plunge the stuff into another machine.

I don't know what happens inside that machine, but crumbly stuff is going in, and at the other side of the machine, sprinkles are shooting out a tube about the size of a firehose and with about the same amount of force.

"Wow!" Greta says. "Look at all that!"

We reach the end and that's it. We've gone around a curve that has put us back in the atrium with all the different rooms. We've received no additional information as to the sprinkles versus jimmies debate, but I'm willing to overlook that because nothing terrible happened.

"The confectionary now?" I ask hopefully. I spun the wheel, it went okay, and that's really about as far as I'd like to push my luck right now.

She takes pity on me and says, "Sure. Maybe we can catch up to Pinky for her second round of ice cream."

We cross the atrium and enter the confectionary. It's huge and set up by style. Gelato is to the left, then soft serve, then scoops. Finally, there's an area called "specialty," which I assume means cow's milk or whatever. If that's not what it means, I'm not sure I want to know about it.

The place smells unbelievably terrific. There's a vanilla baked good kind of smell, which must be the cones themselves. Then there are whiffs of fruit flavors, chocolate, and I don't even know what else, but I suddenly really, really want an ice cream cone more than I want anything else in life.

"What kind do you want?" I ask.

Pinky appears out of nowhere. You'd think this would be impossible, given her size and her conspicuousness, but she's ridiculously stealthy and can somehow pull off a sudden emergence from a crowd.

It's one of the things I like about her.

This reminds me, though, that I haven't yet seen another Mebdarian mutant. My understanding was that, while unusual, they aren't terribly rare to see. Kind of like ginger-haired people and left-handers.

By the way, ginger-haired people are far more likely to be left-handed than anyone else. Did you know that? I knew that. Statistics. Hah.

Also, beware left-handed gingers. They're not the Mebdarian kind of mutant, but they're legit Earth mutants, and capable of more than you'd think.

Pinky takes charge of our frozen treat dilemma.

"The scoops are what you need," she says, driving us toward the scoop shop like a tireless border collie rounding up sheep.

"Scoops it is," Greta laughs. "What do you recommend?"

We get to the board that lists the flavors, and I'm tired just looking at it. I'd guess that everything I can possibly think of is up there, along with a bunch of things I never thought to think of.

"They're all good," Pinky says. "It just depends on what you're in the mood for."

Hang on.

"All of them?" I ask. "You've tried them all?"

"Sure. My youth was not of the misspent variety," Pinky says. "I had priorities."

I nod agreeably. She's an accomplished woman, our Pinky.

"The cherry chocolate chip sounds good," Greta says.

"Good choice," Pinky says. "How about you, Charlie?"

"A fruit flavor, I think," I say. "I'm just not sure which."

"You could go with the one named after me," she says casually.

That gets my attention, as well as Greta's.

"Which one is that?" I ask.

"Pinky Peach. It's peach and passion fruit swirl, with a marshmallow ribbon running through. It's really good."

"Wow," Greta says. "How did you get them to name a flavor after you?"

Pinky shrugs, as if this is no big deal. "Only three people have ever eaten all the flavors. When that happens, they honor the person with a personalized flavor."

"Who were the other two?" I ask.

"Not entirely sure," Pinky answers. "But their flavors are Lucy's Laser Lemon and Dan's Diabetic Dream."

"I bet Dan's flavor doesn't get a lot of takers," I say.

"Are you kidding? It's in the top five most popular. Not only is it delicious, but it has a sexy name."

Pinky and I clearly have different ideas about what makes a sexy ice cream flavor name.

We proceed to put in our orders—mine in a sensible waffle bowl to prevent drippage, and Greta's in a tall, thin sugar cone.

Pinky gets an octuple scoop of Sweet Red Bean mixed with Violent Vanilla. It takes two people to hand it to her, and there has to be more than a gallon of ice cream there. I'm sure this is her second round, too.

We sit down at a small round table at the far side of the confectionary and people-watch while we eat our frozen treats.

"This is incredible," I say after my first blissful taste. It seems like Billy and Nanny have cracked the code on how to pack extra flavor into each gram of ice cream. It's the tastiest ice cream I've ever had.

"Told ya," Pinky says between large bites of ice cream.

"Mine's good, too," Greta says, looking quite pleased with her cherry chip.

I carefully spoon up a bite of my treat, but somehow, defying the laws of physics, my gentle prodding causes half of my ice cream to careen out of the waffle bowl and land on the table in front of me with a sad, squishy thump.

Physics has never been my friend.

"It's still good." Pinky reaches out and grabs the ice cream blob, preparing to drop it back into my bowl for me.

"Uh, that's okay," I say, pulling the remainder of my ice cream close and guarding it with a hand. Even if I had no concerns about table-borne pathogens, I still wouldn't feel good about free-range ice cream returning to my bowl from the pasture.

Pinky shrugs and smashes the fallen ice cream into the top of her cone. "It'd be a shame to waste it."

I decide a good diversionary topic of conversation is in order. "Pinky, why is it we haven't seen any other mutants?"

She swallows a large bite of ice cream, starts to answer, then puts a hand to her head. "Ooh."

"Brain freeze?" Greta asks.

"Yep." Pinky loves them. I can see her relishing the sensation.

We don't know why she likes brain freezes. Maybe, like Mebdarian hush puppies and fried dough, Mebdarian brain freezes are just better.

Pinky shakes her head. "You have seen mutants. You just can't always tell. Not very many of them wear it all on the outside like me. And some of them who do show it prefer to cover it up for cosmetic purposes."

"Why?" Greta asks. "Do people look down on it?"

"Nah. Not really," Pinky says. "But some people's mutations don't show up as awesomely as mine. Like, an extra ear on a forearm or two livers or something. Those aren't things you'd be able to see."

"So even among mutants, you're special," I say.

"Damn right," Pinky says proudly.

"Of course she is," Greta agrees. "We already knew that."

As we eat, Pinky points out people she recognizes and particular spots where she stood or sat while eating Billy and Nana's various products.

Some of these confidences are more interesting than others. Actually, I'm just being nice. None of them are interesting.

We all finish our ice cream at about the same time. Pinky smooths her hands over her hips and outer thighs. "One more round?"

Greta shakes her head and puts a hand to her stomach. "Not for me."

I shake my head.

Pinky shrugs. "All right. I'll come back later. Let's go see how the matchmaking girl is doing."

"Should we check in so soon?" Greta asks.

"Why waste time?" Pinky asks. "We'll be taking off again soon, and if Jon doesn't have someone by then, he'll have to wait until I can get some vacation time."

"When you put it that way, I guess we should hurry," Greta says.

We leave Billy and Nanny's in search of the flamingo bus.

11

I DON'T KNOW if this is just how things work on Mebdar II, or if it's Greta's luck, but either way, we have an interesting evening ahead of us.

When we return to the matchmaking agency, Sloan has managed to arrange for three women to meet Jon.

I had to face certain death and travel into space to find a girl, and Jon Peach gets three of them delivered right to his apartment.

I guess that's what happens when you have Pinky for a sister.

Pinky, of course, must attend this initial meeting, which is described to me as more of an interview than a date. Sloan will attend as well, as facilitator, and Greta and I are invited as well, to give the evening a sort of mix and mingle, cocktail party feel.

I feel like this is all leading to something that's going to be highly interesting and wildly entertaining.

There's this odd feeling in the pit of my stomach. It's not dread. It's not food poisoning. It's not familiar.

I think it's...anticipation. The good kind, not the crippling anxiety type.

Since I don't have anything dressier than pants and a shirt, that's what I wear. I feel like I'll be underdressed, and when I see Pinky and Greta, my feeling is confirmed.

Greta's wearing a pretty, dark green cocktail dress that ends just above her knee. Pinky's wearing a pair of black hip-hugger trousers and a white shirt with short sleeves.

I've never seen her in sleeves. It's a little weird.

Jon greets us at the door of his apartment, looking nice but not overly eager in a casual suit that shows off his good looks.

When his eyes rest on Greta a little too long, I uncharacteristically step forward and greet him heartily.

"Good to see you again!" I exclaim. "This seems like it's going to be a great night."

He looks at me with a faint look of confusion, as if he's trying to remember where he's seen me before.

He recovers quickly. "Ah, yes, it should definitely be interesting."

As he shows us into the apartment, he asks Pinky, "Are you sure we shouldn't have done this at a restaurant or something? I feel a little odd about doing it here."

Pinky shrugs. "We're looking to streamline this process. If any of these women have a problem with how you live, it's better to know it straight off."

"What could be wrong with how I live?" Jon asks, looking around the apartment as if trying to see it as a stranger would. "I keep it tidy and in good repair. It's decorated nicely, but not ostentatiously."

"I hate to say it, but you're a little dull, Jon," Pinky says. "But don't worry. A lot of women like that. Look at Greta, here." She gestures to Greta, then me.

Greta looks about half as startled as I feel about this backhanded but brutal set down.

Jon seems puzzled. I'm pretty sure he still doesn't really believe Greta and I are a thing. As if his mind just can't make the leap.

Honestly, I can't blame him.

I want to, don't get me wrong. I just can't.

We help Jon arrange some snack foods and glasses on a side table. When the doorbell rings, we all look at each other. We all have heightened feelings of excitement, for different reasons.

Jon opens the door and Sloan enters, followed by three women.

At first glance, I'm convinced that Sloan has taken a sampler-platter approach to this meeting. The first woman is tall and dark. The second is small and blond. The third is blue-haired and angry. She walks stiffly, and her face appears to be permanently pressed into a glaring frown.

Yep. That's quite the sampler.

Sloan makes introductions. She glosses quickly over Pinky, Greta, and me before introducing Jon to the three eligible bachelorettes. Then she indicates each of them.

"This is Nancy," she says of the tall one.

"This is Lauria," she says of the blond.

"And this is Mauritza," she says of the angry one.

Jon politely shakes the hand of each of them and manages to say all the right things.

It seems that Jon is pretty smooth.

Minutes after their arrival, we all settle into the living room with our drinks. I've decided to approach this as if I'm a lamp that is currently turned off. I'll be here. I'll observe things. But I don't plan to contribute anything. This seems to be the best possible thing I can do to help things along.

I do want this to be a success. If Pinky doesn't find a wife for her brother, she might have to take time off from the *Second Chance*, and I don't want to see that happen.

Plus, you know, Jon and happy endings and blah blah, whatever.

Jon explains his job, which the bachelorettes all seem to know already. Then they take turns sharing what they do.

"Stockbroker," says Nancy.

"Talent agent," Lauria reports.

"Behavioral therapist," Mauritza says, looking like she just ate a lemon.

"That's interesting," Jon says. "What kind of conditions do you treat?"

"Oh, all kinds," she answers. "But what I see the most is anxiety. It's just so prevalent these days. It's so sad, because it really has a detrimental effect on people's lives."

"Sounds like someone you'd like to know, Charlie," Pinky says.

And now everyone's attention is on me. Great. That's exactly what I didn't want.

"Do you have anxiety?" Mauritza asks.

"I do," I say carefully. "I'm working on it, though."

I keep my answer short in the hopes of returning her attention to Jon.

But Mauritza nods sympathetically. "It's a big battle. Much harder than people who haven't experienced anxiety realize. And that's part of the problem—the lack of understanding."

Suddenly, Mauritza is my favorite in this race. She hasn't, in fact, been angry all this time. She's actually very thoughtful and kind. She just has one of those faces.

"Do you ever experience anxiety, Jon?" I ask, endeavoring to put the spotlight back on him.

Jon purses his lips thoughtfully. "I think everyone does sometimes. I worry for my patients. But fortunately, it isn't something that gets in the way of my life. I'm sorry you have to deal with that, Charlie."

I feel a small zing of success. He actually knows I exist, and even knows my name. And you know, he's kind of a nice guy. I don't get the feeling he's saying that just to look good for the ladies. He really means it.

Aw. Pinky's brother is a Peach.

Now I want him to find a nice woman for his own sake, not just to take his attention away from Greta.

The conversation flows on around me, touching on various topics. All three women seem pleasant, and though I try, I can't tell if any of them are truly interested in Jon or if he's interested in any of them. My vote goes to Mauritza. It's not her fault her resting face looks like she just stubbed her toe. It's what she has inside that matters.

Her character, I mean. Not her internal organs and viscera.

An hour and a half after they arrived, Sloan and the bachelorettes leave. On her way out, Mauritza slips me her card.

I think that's sweet.

After Jon closes the door after them, he leans against it and lets out a long sigh. "That was rough. How did I do?"

"I thought you were great!" Greta enthuses.

Pinky lofts a single thumb. "Solid job, bro. If any of them doesn't like you, then they're just freaking idiots."

Jon grins, making him look even better-looking than usual.

I hope Greta isn't looking.

I sneak a peek at her. Dang it. She's totally looking at him.

Pinky stands. "Well, we're out of here. I'll talk to you tomorrow. We can start planning the wedding."

She points her finger at Jon and makes a click sound. I'm pretty sure this is meant to be encouraging, but if it were me, with that finger pointed at me, I'd definitely develop a case of serious anxiety.

We take our leave. We decide to walk to the bed and breakfast, since it isn't far and the night air is so pleasant. It smells a bit like cotton candy, actually. Yum.

"So what do you think?" Greta asks. "I thought all three of them seemed decent."

"They were okay," Pinky agrees.

"Do you think he likes one?" I ask. "I couldn't tell."

"Oh, he definitely took a shine to someone," Pinky says.

"Really?" Greta sounds surprised. "I didn't pick up on it."

"He's subtle, but I know my brother," Pinky says confidently. "He's smitten."

"It's not Greta, is it?" The words pop out of me like corks that have been packed under extreme pressure.

I didn't mean to say that.

"Of course not," Pinky scoffs.

"Are you going to tell us who?" Greta asks.

"Nope. That's for him to do. He's met the right girl. I approve, and now the rest is up to him."

Pinky seems quite satisfied with the situation. When we arrive at the B&B, though, she doesn't follow us.

"You two go in," she says. "Enjoy all your sleeping. I'm heading back to Billy and Nanny's for another go."

"Maybe you'll be the first person to ever get two flavors named after them," I suggest. Considering how much ice cream she eats, I figure it's the least Billy and or Nanny could do for her.

"This is why I like you, Charlie," she says. "Every now and then, you say something really cool."

She clicks that finger at me, but follows it up with a little kick and a fancy spin, then poses dramatically. As a result, I don't feel intimidated, and have to wonder if she's gearing up for a dance battle.

Some parts of Pinky's life remain a mystery to me.

We spend the next day sightseeing. We ride the puffin bus, the spoonbill bus, the toucan bus, and the pelican bus.

My favorite was the pelican. I don't know why.

Pinky shows us a museum, the Planetary Bust a Move Monument, and the alley where an apparently epic dance battle that changed the course of the planet's development happened.

There's a plaque and a gazebo and everything.

We even happen across a real-time minor dance battle. Pinky doesn't waste any time and just bounces right to the middle, breaks out some amazing moves, and makes everyone else realize that they need to rethink their entire existence.

That's how good she is.

At the end of it all, we hit up Billy and Nanny's again, because Pinky deserves it after her epic moves and patient tour guide treatment. I play it safe and get a banana-flavored, goat yogurt smoothie.

As I get ready for bed that night, I reflect on my experiences on Mebdar II. Of all the planets I've visited, this is my favorite. The abundance of can-do attitude, a tight community, and the belief that differences can be ironed out by dancing has won me over.

It's no wonder it's such a great place, I suppose. This place made Pinky, and she's amazing.

I wonder what Greta's planet is like.

Before we leave Mebdar II, we have a lunch scheduled to meet with Jon and his new girlfriend. Pinky seemed so sure that he'd met the girl of his dreams, but it's been less than two days, and although I one hundred percent believe in Pinky, I have a hard time imagining such a courtship.

Greta, Pinky, and I enter the café where we're to meet Jon and the lucky lady. Upon looking around, we see that they haven't arrived yet. We get a table near a window and order drinks.

I have to admit, this is really exciting. Any minute, Jon's going to come through that door and reveal the winning bachelorette. Even though I have no stake in this, I'm really hoping it's Mauritza.

Then it happens. The door opens. Jon's pulled it open and someone comes through.

It's Sloan. The matchmaker. Her hair is down around her face and she's wearing a pretty pink blouse and a pair of jeans.

Hang on. Did something go wrong? Are we starting over? Will there be another setup with multiple applicants?

I'm confused.

But Sloan's dressed too casually for a work thing, isn't she? And she's looking at Jon with an expression that doesn't seem at all professional.

Ohh.

Well, this is a twist.

I look at Pinky, who is smiling one of the biggest smiles I've ever seen on her face. She's not at all surprised by this.

"Hi again," Sloan says when she arrives at the table with Jon's hand on her waist. "It's good to see you all again."

Greta's wearing an expression of delight, and I can tell she's dying to ask questions but repressing herself. All of her glee nearly leaks right out of her eyeballs. I don't know how she manages to hold it all in. Even her glow is bigger.

We keep it together, though. We follow the lead of the locals and act like this is any other lunch where someone is introducing a new girlfriend.

Sloan is great company. She's funny and articulate, and she and Jon are clearly digging each other.

Pinky's particularly pleasant, though every now and then I catch a hint of smugness in her expression.

It's a nice lunch. Nothing terrible happens. Nothing amazing happens. But it's monumental in its own way. Assuming Jon and Sloan get serious and get married someday, this is a big piece of family history happening right now. I feel all warm and gooey at having been included in it.

Does it make me like part of the family?

I hope so.

Afterward, Pinky and Jon give each other a big hug and

promise to see each other soon, then the three of us return to the bed and breakfast to get our bags.

It's time to go home.

As much as I've enjoyed this trip, I'll be glad to get back to my own bed and my comfortable routine. I also need to check up on Nana. Hopefully she hasn't been thrown into prison or assimilated anyone while I was gone.

You never know with her.

With our bags in hand, we board the elevator to go back to the ship. Finally, my curiosity gets the best of me and I have to ask.

"Do you really think they'll get married?"

Pinky nods. "I give it 80/20 odds. There's a possibility it won't work out, but I think it will. The kenogu feels right. I have a sense for these things. I had the same feeling when I met both of you."

Aw. Now I feel all warm and gooey again.

"So you knew Sloan was the one Jon liked?" Greta asked.

"Oh, yeah. I knew she was the one as soon as I met her. Meeting the three women was just an excuse to get her and Jon into a room together. And tada."

"Wow," Greta says. "That's pretty slick. But you know, I had a fantastic time on your planet. It's a wonderful place."

"Of course it is," Pinky says. "The three of us need to work on some moves, though, for next time. I didn't want to say anything, but I was a little embarrassed that we didn't have a routine worked out for dance battles."

I hadn't realized we'd committed a dance battle faux pas by not having a routine ready. "But I can't dance."

"We'll work on it," Pinky says. "We'll figure something out."

And as surely as I know I can't dance, I believe Pinky will nonetheless figure something out. That's how great my faith in her is—as great as my acknowledgment of my failings.

We step on to the elevator.

Welcome to the Chance 3000, a familiar voice says. *We elevate you because you elevate us.*

Now I'm the one getting a weird sense of kenogu. Of all the things the *Chance 3000* has done, it's never greeted us with its original mid-ride.

I have a bad feeling about this.

We regret to inform you that the Second Chance *is on lockdown. When we arrive, you will be escorted to a holding area where you will stay until further notice.*

I look at Pinky. Is this a prank?

Her expression tells me it isn't.

Greta's eyes have gone wide and round.

Well...crap.

KUNG FU NANA AND OTHER THINGS THAT DIDN'T GO AS EXPECTED

12

THERE ARE SO many things a redshirt worries about. To be sure, I've made great improvements in regard to anxiety and my willingness to try new things. While I'll never have Pinky's supreme confidence, I remain committed to pushing the limits usually set upon my people.

I'm a work in progress.

However, I'm now faced with a unique situation, and I'm unsure of how to approach it.

While Pinky, Greta, and I were on Mebdar II, judging dance battles, eating ice cream, and finding a girlfriend for Pinky's brother, Nana went off the rails.

It was always a risk to bring her aboard the *Second Chance.* Heck, it's always a risk to have anything to do with a Kenny. And cyborg or not, Nana is most definitely still a Kenny. Less so than most of us, since she only has about forty percent of her original parts. So she's forty percent Kenny. But that's still more than enough to wreak havoc in ways that a person who is zero percent Kenny can truly appreciate.

It's with that knowledge and sense of foreboding that I sit down with the ship's captain in his ready room.

I've never even met the captain before, so this is momentous for more than one reason.

Captain Studebaker is tall, lean, and in good shape for a human of sixty years. There's a brightness in his eyes that says not much gets past him but he also has a certain weariness that says he's seen some shit.

"It's good to meet you, Mr. Kenny. I understand you've been on the ship for some time now," he says, toying with a cup of tea but not picking it up.

"Yes, sir," I say. "The ship has become my home. But please, call me Charlie."

He nods seriously. "Okay, Charlie. But only if you call me Slap."

"Slap?" I ask. "That's your name?"

"No, but I always wanted it as a nickname. Maybe if you start calling me that, it will finally catch on."

"Oh. Okay." I'm not sure what to make of this.

Fortunately, the captain—the newly minted Slap—continues with the main focus of our meeting. "I'm afraid there's a problem with your grandmother."

I knew it. As soon as I found out the *Second Chance* was on lockdown, I was certain Nana was the cause.

I should have insisted she come with us down to Mebdar II, where we could keep an eye on her.

"What seems to be the problem, sir? Uh, I mean, Slap." Maybe if I butter him up with his desired nickname, he'll go a little easier on Nana.

He sighs. "I can look the other way on some things. I realize your nana's old and she has the cyborg issue. It's a damn shame when that happens, and I'm not without sympathy. But this kind of thing is too much to overlook."

I feel like he's about to make a pronouncement. And while I don't know a lot about ship captains, I do know that once they've made a pronouncement, they're very reluctant to change it. Much like a parent or a war general.

To try to ward off this point of no return, I rush in. "It's just a pastime for her. I really don't think she gets much money from it. She just enjoys the thrill of canasta."

How many times did I tell her not to gamble on a ship? How many times did I warn her that it was against the law? Lots, that's how many.

But Slap looks puzzled. "What's this about canasta?"

Apparently that's not what he's talking about. Oops. "Uh, nothing," I say smoothly. "I meant something else."

Yep. Smooth.

Slap looks unconvinced.

I decide to practice the art of distraction. "So why's the ship on lockdown?"

Will it work? Slap's expression wavers, as if he's torn between investigating what I said further and moving on with what he intended to say.

"Unfortunately, a guest reported that he woke up to find your nana trying to assimilate him," Slap says.

Yes. Distraction successful.

"Oh, that?" I ask nonchalantly. "It's harmless. She doesn't even have the tools to do it. Assimilating a human takes very specific gear, and it's pretty messy, too."

Saying that second bit probably wasn't helpful. Slap's nose has acquired a scrunch of disgust.

"Regardless of the success of the attempt, the Chance Fleet takes a dim view of cyborgs attempting to assimilate our passengers. It's very bad for business."

"Right," I say. "That's entirely reasonable. But I hope you can take into consideration her side of things."

"Her side?" Slap seems surprised.

"Well, think about it," I say. "She was just an elderly woman making some baked goods when the cyborgs appeared in her kitchen and assimilated her. She didn't ask for that. They programmed her with certain tendencies. It's not like she *wants* to do those things."

He rubs his chin. "So you're saying it's a disability."

"Something like that," I agree. "But also, she's an old lady. I mean, I once knew a woman who carted vegetables around in a stroller and insisted they were her children. Isn't it up to the younger generations to have some kindness and understanding?"

Slap sighs. "I get what you're saying, Charlie. And you have a point. I'm sympathetic to what your grandmother has been through. But the fact remains that I can't have a cyborg on board doing assimilations, even if they're just pretend assimilations. People just don't like that."

"I hear you, Slap," I say in my most fraternal, bro-type way. "And that's exactly why we're headed to Mebdar IV to begin with. Being a retirement planet, they've seen a lot of this kind of thing and are equipped to handle it. But how is Nana supposed to get there, if not on a ship? How about we put her under guard to ensure she doesn't make any trouble? We're almost to Mebdar IV anyway."

I hold my breath.

Slap stands and paces around the ready room. "It's a reasonable request. And since her intended destination is Mebdar IV, that will get her off the ship sooner than if we rendezvoused with a penal ship."

I know we're in a serious situation and all, but his choice of words makes me chuckle.

"What?" he asks.

"Nothing," I say.

"No, something was funny. What?"

"No, it was nothing."

"Tell me," he insists.

"Well...you know. Just the way you said that. Rendezvoused

isn't a word you hear every day, and it kind of sounds like a name. Rondé Vood."

Understanding dawns on his face. "Aha. Rondé Vood and the Penal Ship. I get it." He snickers like a schoolboy. "I don't think we have that one on the lightstream."

"I sure hope not," I say.

Slap's amusement has lightened the mood, and I hope that means he's going to give Nana a break.

"All right," Slap says. "Your grandmother can be confined to her quarters with two assigned guards until we arrive at Mebdar IV. That's only two days away, so we can make the best of it. It's very important, though, that she doesn't make any trouble during that time. If she does, it will become a PR nightmare for the fleet."

"Pinky's very fond of Nana," I say quickly. "I'm sure she'd be happy to help keep an eye on things."

Slap's eyebrows go up. "Is she, now? Well, that would be helpful. Nobody can keep things in line like Pinky."

"She'll help," I say. "I'm sure of it."

"All right, then," Slap says. "It sounds like that's the best possible scenario for all involved. Just make sure you keep that nana of yours under control."

"Absolutely," I agree. "No problem."

Slap and I shake hands, and I confidently leave the ready room.

Once the door closes behind me, I let all that faux confidence evaporate.

I mean, you've seen Nana. You know as well as I do that keeping her "under control" won't be "no problem."

It's going to be all *kinds* of problems.

WHEN I HAVE A PROBLEM, I go to Pinky's bar. Not for a drink. For the advice and help of my friends.

As I enter, the place is a madhouse. Every table is packed. Pinky's behind the bar, mixing drinks like a fiend, slapping them onto trays and in front of guests.

Instead of sitting at the bar, I go behind it. "What can I help with?"

"Two Mendacious Moocows, one Perspicacity Incarnate, a Saturn Surprise, and a Shitweasel."

I pause in the middle of reaching for a glass. "Uh. A Shitweasel? I don't know that one."

Pinky doesn't look at me as she answers. She's too busy crushing lemons with her bare hands. "One part grenadine, two parts club soda, two parts champagne."

"That sounds pleasant enough," I say, grabbing the glass. "Why the name?"

Pinky throws the sad remains of the lemons into the pulper. "I named it after the woman who first asked for that combination. Good drink. Shitweasel of a woman."

Fair enough. We spend the next twenty minutes getting caught up on the backlog of drinks. Finally, when we're keeping pace with the orders, I ask, "Why is it so busy?"

"Oh, it's Discovery Day," Pinky says. "Didn't you know?"

"No. What's Discovery Day?"

She pulls the towel off her shoulder and wipes a wet smear off the bar before tossing the towel back over her shoulder. "It's a Mebdarian celebration of the vastness of the universe and how planets and peoples keep getting discovered. It's about unity."

"And what's better for unity than getting plastered, right?" I venture.

"Exactly. Discovery Day's damn good for business."

"Did you invent it?" I ask. Considering her love for pranking people and her insistence that Mebdarians invented things, it seems like a good possibility.

"Me?" she asks. "Nah. It's like, two hundred years old or something."

I add ice to a glass and nod. "Ah."

She adds, "But if it hadn't been invented long before I was born, I'd have invented it."

I believe her.

"Funny how many people are out already. The lockdown only let up a few minutes ago."

Slap had announced the end of the lockdown while I was on my way to the bar.

"Eh," she says. "We were getting slammed with orders even during the lockdown. Both here and in the dining room. What else are people supposed to do when they're crammed up in their cabins?"

Makes sense. "About the lockdown," I say. "Did you know it's because of Nana?"

"There's not much about this ship I don't know," Pinky says.

I take that as a yes.

"I had a meeting with Slap and promised to help keep Nana under control and under guard until we get to Mebdar IV."

"Slap?" Pinky stops and actually hits me with some eye contact. "You actually agreed to call him that?"

"Seemed like the thing to do. Why?"

"He's always trying to get that name to catch on." She shakes her head.

"Well, what do you call the captain?" I ask.

"Stude. It's a mix of Studebaker and Dude. He doesn't like it."

The name certainly does not have a ring to it. "Anyway," I say, steering the conversation back on course. "Can you help with Nana? Make sure she doesn't make any trouble in the next couple of days? I don't want her getting carted off to a prison or something."

"Sure," Pinky says. "I'll see what I can do. But what are you going to do if she doesn't like Mebdar IV?"

"What do you mean?" I ask.

"Well, what if she wants to go back to Earth or something? If she doesn't want to stay on Mebdar IV, it seems to me you'll have a big problem on your hands."

Yes, indeed. I hadn't quite focused on that angle. "I guess we'll have to hope she likes it there," I say. "Maybe we can talk it up to her. Help her see the benefits of the place."

Pinky nods. "I think it'd be a good spot for her. Plus, it's in my home system, which would make it easy to visit her. Okay. Let's do our best to help Nana Rose fall in love with Mebdar IV."

"I'm sure Greta will help," I say. "And between you and her, I bet you can get Nana settled."

Game on, Nana. Game on.

13

"SORRY, CHARLIE," Nana says.

I've joined her in her cabin. Slap had promised guards, and two of them stood looking less than pleased about being pulled from their regular duties to stand around outside an old lady cyborg's door.

Nana holds her hands in her lap, looking contrite. "I didn't mean to try to assimilate the guy. Sometimes, my mind wanders, and I find myself doing something really cyborg-like. It's in the code. It's not me."

"I know." I pat one of her cold, metal hands. "But people are understandably freaked out. So that's going to mean a couple of quiet days for you before we arrive at Mebdar IV."

"Gus will visit me," she says confidently. "It will be fine. It's not for long."

"That's right," I agree. "We'll be there before we know it."

"Literally, in my case, if my mind wanders again," she says.

"Let's try to keep that from happening," I suggest.

She nods. "That's probably for the best. So how are things with you and Greta?" she asks. "Any hanky panky?"

I'm not sure how literally she means that, and I don't want to know. “We’re good,” I say. “We had a nice time on Pinky’s homeworld. It’s a fantastic place, actually. You know, if you settle on Mebdar IV and I settle on Mebdar II, we’d be neighbors and I could visit you all the time.”

This is my opening salvo in the battle of getting Nana to like the retirement planet.

“That’s a nice thought,” she says pleasantly. “We’ll see what Gus thinks when we get there.”

Gus. Why Gus? She’s mentioned him twice now.

“What does Gus have to do with it?” I ask.

“He’s a shrewd person. A kick-ass canasta partner, too. I’m not sure I’d have much fun there without him.”

Rats. Looks like I’m going to have to get Gus on board with the endeavor, too. Considering the difficult relationship he and Pinky have had, this adds a new degree of difficulty to my mission.

Out of the blue, I imagine the red shirt that’s neatly folded in my closet.

Nope. No. I’m going to stay positive. Pinky and Greta will help. We’ll make this work.

NEEDLESS TO SAY, the elevator ride down to Mebdar IV is fraught with tension.

We have Nana and her unpredictability, and my need for her to like the planet. Then we have Gus. Between you and me, Gus has been cracked for a little while now. The pressures of seeing to the needs of thousands upon thousands of insterstellar travelers along with his need for perfection, and his staunch adherence to rules has done something to him.

Or maybe it was Pinky messing with him that broke his brain.

Regardless of the cause, Gus is a little bit of a loose cannon these days.

It's probably why Nana likes him.

It's also making me nervous about this visit.

Our first hurdle is the elevator. As the doors close, I send Pinky as severe a look as I dare, hoping against hope that the *Chance 3000* won't choose this moment to engage in some shenanigans.

The *Chance 3000* had a key role in ruining Gus, after all. I'm not sure what Gus will do if the elevator insists on a dance party, a moment of contemplation, or goes into night-vision mode.

I hold my breath. I'm doing that a lot lately, it seems. It's probably a bad idea. Hypoxia is no joke. Although, considering the stench thing the elevator did when we went down to Mebdar II, holding my breath is a legit defensive move.

I breathe, though, because of the hypoxia thing and focus on Greta. Hopefully, her kenogu will get us over this first hurdle.

Welcome to the Chance 3000.

Mentally, I make the scream of the damned.

Gus tenses, and a wild look appears in his eyes.

Please enjoy your ride.

I'm waiting. What will it be this time? Will the elevator hurl obscenities at us in a bewildering array of planetary languages? Make us recite poetry? Require us to solve a riddle?

What?

What?

What?

The anticipation is killing me. Not literally. I shouldn't bandy a word like that around, considering my background. But waiting to see what the elevator will do is a rough gig.

Then the doors open and as we step out, I feel a crushing avalanche of relief.

That was a close one.

The elevator has deposited us in a somewhat unusual place. Rather than being outdoors or in some transit station, we're in a room of overstuffed couches and perfectly smooth, rubbery floors. I see no pointed edges or tripping hazards anywhere.

A knot that I always carry around in my chest loosens slightly.

This planet was, after all, my intended destination when I left Earth. I feel kind of like I've come full circle with my intentions, even though I'm now here for Nana and not myself.

Right. We have a job to do here. I look to Greta then Pinky for a morale boost. Together, the three of us can do this.

"It's a little boring," Nana says, looking around. "But inoffensive. Don't you think so, Gus?"

We all look to Gus. Before he cracked, he'd have said something very agreeable and extremely polite.

He shrugs.

Wow.

This is not the Gus I know.

"Where's the tour guide, Charlie?" Nana asks, sounding cranky. "You promised a tour guide."

Pinky steps in to help me out. "No worries, Nana Rose, we're on a retirement planet. We get to be laid back. People might run a few minutes later. It's good."

"Well…if you say it's good, I guess it must be." Nana doesn't sound exactly agreeable, but her faith in Pinky is reassuring.

I look around for the person I previously spoke to who assured me she'd meet us for a tour. She'd sounded like a pleasant, older lady with a good sense of humor, and I think Nana will like her.

The young woman who bounces into the room isn't the person I'm expecting, but she plants herself in front of us and grins. "Hi! I'm Peaches, and I'll be taking you on your tour. Welcome to Mebdar IV. I'm sure you'll like it."

Pinky's the first to speak. "Oh, hell no. You're not a peach. I'm a Peach."

This is not the particular line in the sand I'd care to draw. I edge close to Pinky and whisper frantically under my breath,

"Just go with it. We all know you're the real Peach. This is for Nana, remember?"

Pinky's mouth tightens, then she crosses her arms over her chest but says nothing more.

I try to cover. "You're not Ms. Loudencamp, are you? You don't sound like the person I talked to on the phone."

Peaches smiles. "No, she's my boss. But she got called out and asked me to look after you. Don't worry. I'm a five-star rated tour guide."

"There are stars for that?" Greta asks.

"Yep." Peaches nods. "Guiding tours is a critical thing here."

I guess I can see how that would be true. "Well, it's nice to meet you, Peaches. I'm Charlie."

I introduce the other members of our party.

"It's so nice to meet you all," Peaches says. "We're going to have some fun. I really think you'll like it here."

Nana says, "I'll be honest, Peaches. From what I've seen so far, I'm not impressed."

Peaches' smile dims. "Have you seen more than this?" She uses her hands to indicate our surroundings.

"Nope. But I form opinions quickly. And I already know that my grandson there was planning to come live here, which is a negative in my book."

I'm stunned by this unexpected, apparently random insult from my nana. "Gee, thanks, Nana."

Gus speaks up. "I'm with her. The boy is useless."

I stare at him.

"Well, things went wrong for me only after you arrived," he points out.

Yeah, okay. He has a point.

Peaches rallies and cranks the wattage of her smile back up. She takes my arm, startling the heck out of me. "Well, he has better taste than you know, then. I promise, you're going to like it here."

"Be careful making promises to a cyborg," Pinky warns. "They're very, very literal and dislike disappointment."

This doesn't deter Peaches. "I'm not a five-star guide for nothing."

She hugs my arm to her and I feel very, very, strange about it. I look to Greta, who appears to be having some feelings of her own about it.

What's going on here?

As Peaches leads us out to our first tour stop, I have a feeling that this trip is either going to be really special or horrifically awful.

Guess which one I'm betting on, given the statistical odds.

I'LL BE HONEST. I like Mebdar IV. Peaches takes us on a leisurely walk, all the while holding on to my arm. I'm rolling with this, as it's probably some sort of local custom, but the prolonged contact with another person is definitely an oddity for me.

"One of the great things about Mebdar IV is that you never have to go outside," Peaches explains as we stroll down a corridor. "You can if you want to, and we do encourage outdoor activities, but everything is connected via interior walkways. This way, every path has a sturdy handrail, seamless floors to avoid tripping hazards, and protection from ultraviolet radiation."

"Plus," she adds, "it protects you from the weather. Sadly, every now and then, a cyborg gets hit with lightning. But here, that can easily be prevented."

She beams at Nana then at me, as if she's just scored a major point.

Does she get paid by commission or something? She seems so darn eager to please. Or maybe she just genuinely believes that this planet is an ideal haven.

Greta's looking at us again, and I try to casually tug my arm away while Peaches is pointing at the shock-absorbent flooring, which was designed to cushion a person in the event of a fall.

It's a nice safety feature, but I'm having no luck with the escape. Peaches has a death grip on my forearm.

Pinky asks, "So are all the old people locked up in one place?"

A pained expression crosses Peaches' face. "Well, we don't lock them up. I mean, unless it's necessary and approved by both the citizen's physician and case manager. But we have numerous different homes, both locally and farther away. Citizens can travel to other communities via the subway. Mostly, unless they have family in a distant community, they stay within their own community."

"What defines a community?" Nana asks.

I hope she's asking for academic purposes and not planning-stages-for-a-cyborg-insurrection purposes.

"I'm glad you asked," Peaches says, beaming. "Our community is called Ridgeway, and we have a very eclectic grouping of people who like variety. Each of our homes has a different focus, which helps people be closest to those they have the most in common with, while also being able to enjoy the variety of the community as a whole."

The way she says that, I can tell she's said it a lot of times. There's a cadence to her words, as if she's speaking song lyrics or something. It has the distinct feel of a spiel.

Gus speaks up for the first time, surprising me. Mostly, he just glares at everyone, so I hope this means he's loosening up.

I don't like this new, tense version of Gus.

He asks, "So what are the focuses of the homes in Ridgeway?"

Peaches beams at him as if he's said something really amazing. She does a lot of beaming. She's like a floodlight that doesn't turn off. "I'm so glad you asked! We have one that's a bit of an artist's colony. We have a one that's for sports and fitness enthusiasts, one for nature lovers, three for performance and entertainment, a place for those who like to cook, one for people who like to do handcrafts, a home for those who like to play cards—"

At the word "cards," Nana lights up. Literally. Her cybernetic face implants activate, her red eye is glowing, and she has all these blue lights that have gone bright.

"Cards?" she repeats.

"Yes, it's a popular home," Peaches confirms.

"Do they play canasta?" Nana asks.

"Oh yes, of course."

"Take us there," Nana says. "Take me to their leader."

Peaches' expression clouds. "Well, they don't have a leader. Unless you count Myra, who tends to organize the weekly games."

"I want to meet this Myra," Nana states.

"Um, okay," Peaches says, looking at Gus then at me for some kind of help.

Hah. She's in for a surprise. She's the one I'm looking to for help. I am entirely useless.

Maybe when she figures that out, she'll let go of my arm. It's just darn awkward at this point. I mean, I know I should be flattered or something, because she's a very pretty, sentient creature who seems to have taken a shine to me. But my head is not so easily turned by mere sentience and good looks.

Peaches is no Greta Saltz. There's only one woman I want to cling to my arm, and it's Greta.

I don't want to be rude and risk Nana's chances of getting accepted as a citizen, though, so I persevere.

It's what we Kennys do best: squeeze our eyes shut and ride it out.

Peaches continues to patter on about the amenities available to citizens, such as physical therapy, a variety of classes and hobbyist groups, and top-notch medical care.

It sounds great—it really does. I'm reminded of why I almost moved here, and feel a little wistful. Such a bubble-wrapped existence sure would be comfortable.

I really want Nana to decide to stay here and become a citizen. Not just so I can visit her here, but because I think it's a great place for a Kenny.

"What about cyborgs?" Nana asks on the way to the card-playing home—"Aces High," they call it.

Peaches says, "I'm so glad you asked about that!"

She says that a lot. If I didn't know better, I'd suspect she was a cyborg programmed to say it.

Peaches goes on, "We have doctors who specialize in the unique care required for cyborgs, so you'll have excellent care. We have many cyborg citizens, and they are very happy. I can arrange for you to meet a few, if you like."

"That's not what I meant," Nana says. "I meant, how do you protect against a cyborg invasion? Especially considering you have so many of us. Seems like we could do an inside job on this place, easy."

If this disturbs Peaches, she doesn't let on. I get the feeling she's heard this before.

She smiles. "As you correctly point out, we do have to take special precautions. We have devices that squash any cyborg beacons, and prevent communication on cyborg channels. We also have a field set up around the planet that can function as a mass EMP for any arriving ships. So we're perfectly safe against invasion."

Nana visibly shudders at the mention of an EMP. Otherwise, she seems unfazed.

"Are there dance battles here?" Pinky asks. "On Mebdar II, we have dance battles. Epic ones."

"We tend to frown on that," Peaches says. "We've had too many broken bones. We do offer senior yoga classes, though."

I'm pretty sure I hear Pinky mutter something about being a waste of a Mebdarian planet.

We arrive at the Aces High home, and at first glance, it looks like most retirement homes you'd find on Earth. The walls have been painted light yellow, and there's some boring wall art as well as some uninspired flower arrangements.

Suddenly, I want to take a nap.

"Peaceful, isn't it?" Peaches asks, cheerful. "It doesn't get very loud in the common areas, and there's no part of the building that gets an inordinate amount of traffic. We like to keep things on a calm, even keel for our guests."

This sounds quite nice to me, but Pinky grimaces, and this time I hear Nana mutter something about "boring, old-ass people."

I'll admit it, this discourages me. I really need her to like this place.

"Just imagine," I say, hoping to redirect Nana's attention to something positive. "You could play cards here all the time."

Nana shoots Peaches a look. "What's the policy on gambling here?"

Peaches looks surprised. "Gambling? Well, our citizens are all adults, and of course they're welcome to have some fun making some wagers on their games."

Yeah, Mebdar IV clearly isn't prepared for what Nana can wreak on them, but I'm going to pretend I don't know that because Mebdar II's future problems are just that—their problems.

Haha. I'm kind of being a jerk, and it's fun.

Gus mutters something about needing to use the water closet and stomps off.

I really can't get used to the change in him. Dude needs some massive stress relief.

Or...maybe this is him releasing stress. Maybe a lifetime of being polite, helpful, and conciliatory is what cracked his gasket and now all that pent-up rage is hissing out, like a tire leak.

Something to think about, I guess.

An elderly man turns a corner and nearly walks right into Pinky.

"A mutant!" he exclaims, and I prepare myself for a scene.

Not everyone treats mutants kindly.

But then my memory latches on to that voice, and I realize it's a familiar one. I shift to look around Pinky. This causes some ungainly shuffling, thanks to having Peaches still attached to my arm like some kind of overly enthusiastic, attractive parasite.

Actually, when I think about her that way, she reminds me of my cousin's old girlfriend back in New France.

That thought gives me the wherewithal to firmly grasp Peaches' hand and remove it from my arm. I don't even care if she thinks I'm rude.

Greta swoops in and hip checks Peaches out of the way. But it isn't me she's looking at. It's the elderly man who began this scenario.

"Waldorf!" Greta exclaims, grabbing his hands in greeting. "It's so good to see you!"

Then she freezes. "Uh, it is Waldorf, isn't it? Not...Statler?"

Waldorf's brother, as you will recall, is far less likeable. As in, not at all likeable. As in, he's a whacked-out asshole.

"Of course it's me, my dear girl!" Waldorf says. "Either that, or my piss pot of a brother got a hell of a lot nicer. How have you three been?"

"Fine," I say.

"Good," Greta says.

Pinky says, at the same time Greta and I speak, "Eh."

Waldorf's gaze falls on Nana. "Oh, are you thinking of moving here?"

Nana shrugs. "I'm checking it out. How's it working out for you?"

"I love it here," he says. "I don't have to do my own cleaning or laundry, and if I'm told to do something I don't want to, or don't do something I do want to, I pretend I'm senile. It's great."

Nana looks intrigued. “Really? I do like the sound of that.” She glances at Peaches. “You should have led with that. Actually, I think you can go now. We’ve got this.”

Peaches blinks several times in rapid succession. “Uh...that’s not...I mean...”

Pinky fixes Peaches with a look. “Hey. You heard Nana Rose. Get lost. She’s going to be more likely to move here if you aren’t around.”

Ouch. Now that’s a burn. I don’t know whether Pinky intended to deliver such a wicked set down or if she was simply being her usual blunt self, but the end result was kind of hardcore.

Peaches throws a desperate look at me, but I pull a really cool move.

I mean really cool. Like, the coolest thing I’ve ever done. Even more than the time I whacked a blagrook.

I meet Peaches’ beseeching look and put my arm—the one she had latched on to—around Greta’s shoulders.

Score one for Charlie Kenny.

I think that gives me a total lifetime achievement score of one. But it’s a start.

Peaches shuffles away, and none of us is sorry to see her go.

“Stupid fake Peach,” Pinky spits out.

Waldorf nods solemnly. “Don’t let that chipper persona fools you. That Peaches is a viper.”

“Really?” I’d thought her merely annoying.

Waldorf nods again. “Oh yeah. She makes sure people take their meds on time and comes to your room to see if you want to join in activities. Like I don’t already know if I want to play shuffleboard or not.”

“Maybe I should hit her next time I see her,” Nana says.

“Probably not a good idea,” Waldorf says. “I mean, it happens sometimes, but if there’s a pattern, they’ll figure you out, and then you’ll only get vanilla pudding for a month. No chocolate. No lemon. No sweet, tasty butterscotch. Not even tapioca. Just vanilla."

"Sounds like a fair trade," Nana says.

"Some days," he admits. "There's only so much of that super cheerful stuff people can take first thing in the morning. But I don't recommend starting out that way."

Nana sighs. "Fine. Why don't you show me what you like about this place?"

I feel weird about listening to a couple of elderly people strategically plan their disobedience, but I figure I don't have the right to judge them until I get to be their age.

Waldorf ushers us around the home, showing us the reception area, the common room, the cafeteria, the therapy room, and so forth. Without Peaches in tow, our collective mood lightens and suddenly this feels like another adventure. A low-key one, but still an adventure.

Gus hasn't caught up with us by the time we get to the card room, so Greta goes to look for him. That leaves Pinky, Nana, Waldorf, and me watching a spirited game of pinochle.

I'm so glad they were playing pinochle. Because now I get to say pinochle. When I was a kid and read the name before I'd heard it, I thought it was pin-otch-el. Imagine my childish glee in learning that it's actually pronounced pee-knuckle.

It still gives me a giggle. Sometimes words are fun.

Nana leans in close to Waldorf and asks, "How's the canasta circuit? I was supposed to meet a Myra, but she must be taking a nap or something."

Waldorf takes a moment to think about it before answering. "Canasta is popular, but not very organized. Poker's the hot game right now."

"How are the betting stakes?" Nana asks. "Does a lot of money change hands?"

He shrugs. "Usually not so much money as sugar packets or

toothpicks. Every now and then the ladies get wild and do some penny-ante games."

Nana blows out a breath. "I don't know if that means it's hopeless or that they're ripe for conquest. I'm pretty sure Myra will be no match for me."

"Canasta conquest, I hope you mean," Waldorf says. "Not the bigger kind."

"We'll see," she answers tersely, then squares her shoulders.

Actually, they're pretty darn square already. But she lifts her elbows and suddenly looks more menacing. "So what is there to really like about this place? Why would I want to stay?"

"People here are cool," Waldorf says thoughtfully. "What I like most is that it's the least judgmental place I've ever seen. And I've traveled a lot."

"What do you mean by nonjudgmental?" Pinky asks.

I wonder if she's looking for examples or asking about the meaning of the phrase, because I'm not sure Pinky can imagine the world without her scathing judgment.

"Well, we're old, right?" Waldorf asks. "People let us be. If I want to go to the cafeteria and eat dinner in my underwear, then dang it, nobody's going to give me trouble about it. If I have ice cream for breakfast, nobody cares. It's not like I need to worry about my long-term health." He spreads his arms wide. "This is freedom, baby. You can be whatever you want to be here."

Nana looks at him for a long moment. "Now that's an argument worth listening to. I like it. I get judged everywhere I go. 'She looks evil,' people will whisper when I walk by. Children will cling to their parents. Or if I get on a bus, people might scream about how the cyborg invasion has finally arrived. It gets old. Even my dear old friend Mrs. Dubstep prefers to stay out of arm's reach when she comes for tea."

"See?" Waldorf asks. "It's perfect. Nobody here will care about your being a cyborg, so long as you don't do anything threatening. I have a couple of cyborg friends at the cooking home, and they're decent enough."

"The cooking home?" I ask. Having eaten Nana's food, I know firsthand what a bad idea this is.

"Yeah," Waldorf says. "Word to the wise—never visit them over there, or you'll end up having to taste something." He shudders. "Learned that lesson the hard way. But otherwise, they're fine."

I eye Nana in case she's picked up on the fact that we're talking about how bad cyborg cooking is, but she's alertly watching the card play, so I think we dodged that one.

"All right," Nana says. "You've got my attention. Sell me."

Waldorf screws up his face in thought. "The mashed potatoes here are the best. Never any lumps, and super buttery. Sometimes we have talent nights, for real cash prizes. Oh, and we get a lot of celebrity visitors. They like to do publicity shoots here, so they come and meet some folks, hand out some presents, and take pictures with us. I got a picture with Popo Mwah last week. Pretty sweet."

"The musician?" I ask.

"Is there another Popo Mwah?" he asks. Not sarcastically, but for real.

"Not that I know of."

Waldorf shrugs. "It's nice here. I think you'd like it. If you tried it out and didn't like it, you could always leave again."

"That's true," Nana says. "I could see if I can get a good canasta circuit built, and if it doesn't work out, move on. I like it. I like it a lot."

My heart lifts, full of hope.

Hope is a nice feeling, by the way. I mean, you know that, of course, but I'm more of a connoisseur of the feelings dread and fear, and hope is such a delightful change.

This dichotomy between hope and dread is brought to my

particular attention when I hear a crash, a massive boom, and the floor shakes.

Oh, no.

I don't need time to think through what this might be. I just know that fate has, once again, come my way, and we're going to have to fight our way out.

"Kenogu," Pinky says grimly. "Nana Rose, grab Charlie. I'll get my punching fists ready."

She then curls her hands into fists. "Ready."

14

One doesn't simply repel a cyborg invasion. Not when you're a Kenny.

One repels a cyborg invasion—or at least tries to—with a cyborg nana, a girl with statistically impossible good luck, and a badass mutant.

At least, that's how I roll.

Well, I mean, it's how I hope I can roll this. Between you and me, I have worries about Nana's loyalties. Plus, Greta's still off with Gus somewhere. I don't feel good about that at all, since I really need to be in her luck radius right now.

Since we need her luck and because we want to make sure she's safe, finding Greta is our first priority.

Every so often, Nana pauses and gets a faraway look on her face. "They're outside this building now, ground floor."

She turns as if to go join them, but Pinky tugs on Nana's arm. "Come on, Nana Rose, you're with us, not them. You've got to be bigger than your programming, remember?"

Nana blinks. "Right. Yes. We have to get Charlie to safety."

Aw. She's thinking about me and my well-being. I feel all warm and fuzzy.

"He's useless, you know," Nana adds.

Pinky doesn't exactly agree, but she doesn't disagree, either, which frankly, kind of annoys me and completely negates my warm fuzzies.

Hopefully, she simply decided that arguing this particular point wasn't a priority at the moment.

"Is there any way for you to figure out where Greta is?" I ask Nana.

"Not without going into the past and slipping her some kind of tracking device," Nana says. "Which I can't do."

Why didn't she just say no? This pointless pontification is not useful in the midst of a crisis situation.

"Hang on," I say, stopping in my tracks. "Let's not get on the elevator. Wherever Greta is, she probably wants to find us, right?"

Pinky and Nana nod.

"And they always say that if you're lost, you should stay in one place to let rescuers find you. We're not lost, but if Greta wants to find us, she will, and if we stay still, she'll be able to do that faster."

Nana's red eye blinks slowly as she processes this hypothesis. "Eh," she says. "It's as good an idea as any. Plus, it means I don't have to do anything."

"I hate doing nothing," Pinky growls, looking like she wants to bite through the elevator doors. "Doing nothing is my least favorite activity."

"Okay," I say quickly. "You come up with a plan for you, Nana, Greta, and I to escape this building."

"And me," a voice behind us says.

We turn to see Waldorf. He waves. "Hello. Still here."

Yeah, we're kind of jerks for forgetting about him so quickly.

"Of course you too," I say, as if I knew he'd been there all along. "But I see you as more of an anchor person than a hands-on sort."

Did he buy that? I peek at him.

He shrugs. “Whatever, kid. I’m just lucky you two came along. You’ll get me out of whatever this is.”

Two? There are three of...oh, ah ha. Right. Waldorf just put me in my place.

He’s a wily old sack of potatoes.

That’s a phrase Greta taught me. It isn’t mean. Don’t worry.

One of the elevators makes a *ding* sound, and the doors slowly slide open.

Very slowly. If I weren’t staring right at it, I wouldn’t know it was happening.

As the tiny crack widens, I try to peer through it.

Oh my god, how can doors be this slow?

“This is stupid,” Pinky declares. She steps up and yanks the doors apart. There’s a loud *bang* and I’m pretty sure we won’t be taking this elevator back down.

“Charlie! Pinky! I’m so glad to see you!” Greta rushes out of the elevator with her arms open.

I know what you’re thinking. She’s going to run out, I’m going to open my arms, and she’s going to go hug Pinky. Classic comedy. It’s a natural, right? But I’m ahead of this. I keep my arms at my sides because I know how this plays out, too. I watch movies on the lightstream.

Greta slams into my chest and wraps her arms around me.

Okay, I got that one wrong.

“Nana!” she says over my shoulder. “You’re here, too! And I’m glad we’ll have Waldorf with us.”

“Of course I’m with them. What did you think, that I was behind all this?” Nana asks.

“Well...” Greta ducks her head.

“Enough chitchat,” Pinky orders. She hits the elevator button, but it doesn’t make a sound and nothing happens.

“I think the elevators have been turned off. Or else they’ve all shut themselves off in terror after you attacked the first one,” Nana says.

"Stairwell it is, then," Pinky says. "Let's go."

We follow her.

"Did you find Gus?" I ask Greta.

"No," she says. "It's so weird. It's like he disappeared."

Nana pauses and starts to turn around.

I put a hand on her wrist. "Nana, you're staying with us, remember? No joining the invasion."

Nana faces me. "Right. Sorry. I keep getting commands to rejoin the collective. It's very persuasive."

Greta takes Nana's hand. "We'll stick together."

Waldorf grabs Greta's other hand. "Don't leave me out. I'm not a cyborg or a mutant. I'm just an old dude."

Greta's all out of hands now. Dang it.

Well, I'll just stick to Pinky.

She opens the door to the stairwell. Immediately, moaning and howling assault my ears.

"Uh, we have a problem," Pinky says.

Hundreds of old people are hurrying down several flights of stairs. And by hurrying, I mean barely scuffling along and mostly standing still.

It's packed, like a bunch of cows in an overcrowded pasture.

"This won't work," Pinky says. "I can't just start throwing old people. That's not cool, even for me."

She closes the door.

"No elevator and no stairs," Greta says. "Now what?"

"There's the fire escape," Waldorf offers.

Pinky points at him. "Lead the way, Waldorf."

We troop through the halls, which I suppose are so empty because everyone is in the stairwell.

Waldorf leads us down a long, straight hall, then takes a few quick turns that puts us right at the end of the building. There are windows and a nice view, but I'm not really interested in the view at the moment.

"Um," I say. It's not the best way to start a sentence. Not bold or confident. But it's pretty par for the course, for me. "Why are we standing at an exterior wall?"

As far as I can tell, there's no exterior staircase running down the building. All I see is what looks like a weird, industrial balcony.

"Can you open this up?" Waldorf asks Pinky.

"You bet. Stand back." Pinky steps up, grabs the long, metal handle that's been formed on the door, which appears to be a block of solid metal with no seams.

It looks like it was made to stop a bomb.

Pinky lets out a mighty roar and rips the door open. First it comes open at the seam, then it rips right off the hinges.

She drags it a few steps away and drops it with a deafening clang. "There. Now what?"

"Not exactly what I meant, but it got the job done," Waldorf says. "Now we'll have to decide order. It will only hold three of us at a time."

"Charlie, Greta, and Nana Rose, you go first," Pinky says without hesitation.

When Pinky rips a steel door down and tells you to get going, you don't argue. You just do it.

Besides, her solution is the best one I can see as well. Having Greta with me will help keep my kenogu from bringing a horde of cyborgs upon us, and having Nana gives us one strong member. And Pinky takes a lot of room, so having her go with only one other person makes the most sense.

Poor Waldorf. He's just kind of incidental right now. I know how that feels.

I step onto the fire escape, and immediately dislike it.

Are you familiar with those motorized chair things that are stuck to walls to help old people down stairs? They just kind of sit in it, and very slowly proceed up the wall? Well, that's what this fire escape is like.

I guess it makes sense, sort of, given that it's attached to a retirement home, but I really wish I weren't standing on a metal open-air balcony that will slowly descend three stories down.

Back in the days before I met Greta, this would have been a sure thing for me. Certain death. But now, things are different. I've faced a lot of stuff and haven't died. I'm going to suck it up and try to survive this, too.

I've come a long way, baby.

As we descend, I become aware of a high, whining sort of sound. Is the lift breaking? But then I realize it's me, and I stop. I know Nana had to hear it, with her enhanced systems and all, but I hope Greta didn't notice.

It wasn't super loud, at least.

We descend agonizingly slowly. In a way, the lack of speed is good, but it sure does prolong the ride and the stomach-dropping view that comes along with hanging off the side of a building.

Finally, we arrive at the bottom and I let out a small breath of relief. The fire escape lift heads back up for Pinky and Waldorf.

"Uh oh," Nana says.

I hate those two sounds put together. They're very small, yet they tend to be the harbinger of terrible things.

"There's a contingent of three cyborgs coming this way," Nana says. "They'll get here before Pinky does."

"But I don't want to be assimilated!"

I am so, so glad this particular wail came from Greta and not me.

I merely thought it inside my head.

"No worries," Nana says. "We got this."

I don't feel like that's true.

Nana begins disconnecting some hoses and shoving them at Greta and me. "Here."

I look at the hoses in my hands. "Uh. What?"

Nana hisses out an impatient sound. It's all the more insulting because she doesn't actually breathe. She's just doing that to let me know how useless I am.

"Poke those somewhere. In your waistband, in your mouth, up your nose, I don't care. Just make them appear to be part of you," she says. "Hurry."

Feeling like the biggest idiot who ever lived, I stick one end of a hose in my pants pocket, and put the other in my ear. Not too far, though. Ear canals are more fragile than you think. Be careful when you clean your ears. You're not supposed to actually insert anything in there.

But this is a desperate time.

I'm not sure what to do with the other hose I have, but the cyborgs are almost here, so I jam one end under the collar of my shirt and the other in my mouth.

I look at Greta. She's stuck both of hers in her ears and under a piece of elastic on her blouse. It's cute. The way the hoses bend, they're making a heart shape around her face.

Aww. She's even adorable in the middle of a cyborg invasion.

Nana takes charge. She confronts the incoming cyborgs. "This building is under control. Move on to the next."

They don't budge. One of them says, "We have orders to assist with this building."

"And I have orders to kick your asses if you waste resources. Go to the next building."

My nose itches. Well, it's not so much of an itch as it is a tingling sort of burn that indicates the imminent arrival of a sneeze. Because of course I'm one of the small group of people who experience photic sneeze reflex when I'm in bright light.

I try to hold it in, but a photic sneeze will not be denied.

Achoo! The violence of the sneeze makes my hoses pop out of my mouth and ear. Quickly, I put them back in.

"What was that?" the lead cyborg demands.

Nana waves a dismissive hand at me. "Never mind them. They're new. Damn near useless, too. Had to do everything myself."

Will they buy that? Surely they won't.

But the lead cyborg relaxes slightly. "New assimilants are the worst," he says. "All right, moving on."

And they do.

"I pity the cyborgs if they ever decide to assimilate you for real," Nana says to me. "I really do."

I can hardly take umbrage. She's right. I'd be a disaster of a cyborg, constantly popping circuits and blowing fuses.

I look up at the building and see Pinky and Waldorf descending. I'm not sure, but she's moving around in an unusual way, and...yeah. Yeah, she's dancing.

Because she's Pinky Peach, and if she wants to boogie on a fire escape while fleeing a cyborg invasion, then that's what she's going to do.

They reach the bottom and I heave a sigh of relief. I'm eager to get going. I feel like we're just standing around like sitting ducks.

I mean, sitting around like...never mind.

A cyborg scream shatters my sense of relief and makes me wheel around. There's a really big cyborg coming our way and something's wrong with it. Its movements are spasmodic and the sound it's making is a horrible metallic screech.

"She's got a virus," Nana says, clucking her tongue. "That's always nasty. She's not going to listen to reason. Better stand back, kids."

Nana raises her arms like a kung fu fighter.

Out of nowhere, a screaming ball of fury arrives, tackling the cyborg who has run amok.

"It's Gus!" Greta exclaims. She's forgotten to take the hoses out of her ears, and in spite of everything, I laugh.

What else can I do?

For starters, I hand my hoses back to Nana. She might need those for something.

Gus is screaming a litany of profanity the likes of which have never been experienced by mere mortals. I feel like the skin is literally flaying off my ears in response to his noxious tirade.

He's produced a mallet from somewhere and is pounding the run-amok cyborg in the head, over and over, until her head is relatively flat.

Or maybe it's a hammer. What's the difference? The thing Gus is holding has a much larger head than a typical hammer, but it looks to be made of metal and wood, so I'm stymied as to what to properly call the thing.

But I guess that's not the point.

"Gus," I say. When he doesn't answer, I say more loudly, "Gus!"

He looks up with a terrible rage in his eyes, but when he sees me, it clears. His body goes from all lines and angles to a softer, more roundy shape.

He's become Gus again. I can see it. For the first time in weeks, he has an earnest look on his face. "Oh, hello, Mr. Kenny." He bows crisply to each of us, and he acknowledges Greta and Nana as "Ms. Saltz" and "Madam Cyborg," respectively.

Pinky and Waldorf arrive.

"Damn, Gus, you really bashed that 'borg. Nice work!" Pinky raises a hand, and Gus flinches as if he's about to get smacked.

Then he realizes what she's doing and he brightens like a supernova. He gives Pinky a high five like he's just accomplished a life goal.

"You're okay, dude," Pinky says, then gives him a thumbs-up.

I'm touched. I feel like I've witnessed something truly special.

Nana interrupts. "We're still in the middle of an invasion. Mind if we get going?"

"You got it, Nana Rose," Pinky agrees. "Let's get the weak ones to a safe spot, then you and I can go do some smashing."

We begin to hurry toward the elevator that will take us back to the *Second Chance.*

The sky darkens.

We look up and Waldorf says, "Uh oh."

Red and blue satellites have gone up. Thousands of them.

"What is it?" Greta asks.

"It's the backup defense, in case the cyborg EMP in orbit doesn't work. The atmospheric EMP grid will knock out any circuits that are attached to biological matter." Waldorf's staring at the sky. "I've never seen it go up before."

"But that's good, right?" Greta asks.

I look at Nana, and she looks at me. We both know it's most definitely not good for her.

"It's okay, Charlie," she says. "I had a long run for a Kenny. And even though I give you a hard time, I'm proud of you. I'm glad you're the one who will survive me."

She leans in and gives me a hug. In this moment, she seems more like my pre-assimilation Nana than she ever has. The hug almost feels like her old hugs. I can almost smell the scent of not-horrible baked goods on her.

The moment stretches, and I see Greta's expression change to terrible understanding, and Pinky just looks terribly, terribly sorry.

Then Nana goes stiff and falls over.

15

THE MOOD of Mebdar IV is jubilant, with elderly people saying "yay" and clapping their hands briefly before going back to whatever they were doing before.

Greta, Pinky, Gus, Waldorf, and I do not celebrate. We're not sure what to do, really. We stand around my cold, silent nana until the cyborg cleanup crew arrives.

Apparently, under a treaty ordinance between the cyborgs and the Mebdarian system, any thwarted invasions require the invading force to clean up the mess, with no further funny business.

The cyborgs, being so binary, actually honor this ordinance.

They say nothing to us as they put Nana on an antigrav cart and take her away. It feels wrong, but what else can I do? I can't leave her on the planet, and I sure can't take her back to the *Second Chance.*

I'll have to take solace in her last words.

It's not like I'm not used to this kind of tragedy. It's woven into my DNA.

Gus swings into action, getting a drink for Greta and offering me a handkerchief, which I politely decline.

Never accept someone else's handkerchief. You never know where it's been, or what it might be infected with.

Waldorf gives us all a fond farewell before returning to his home for a mandatory head count.

Gus ushers us to the elevator and up to the ship, fussing over us in his own special way.

It's kind of comforting that things are back to normal now.

I guess.

It's hard to feel good about it, though.

We leave the Mebdarian system, and it's like none of the stuff on Mebdar IV ever happened. Guests arrive on the ship, visit places, and leave again. Pinky serves drinks in the bar. Greta serves as brand ambassador.

Three weeks later, I'm still working on getting back to normal. I'm trying to remember how much fun Greta, Pinky, and I had before Nana arrived on the ship, and trying to get back to that.

But all of the Mebdar IV stuff did happen, and I can't forget that. It clings to me.

We battled the cyborg union to get Nana's implants fixed, and we went on to battle blagrooks with her. We even starred in a movie with her—which will be released next spring, so keep your eye out for the promos.

I feel like a chapter of my life has closed, and I don't know what to do. Even my work fails to comfort me.

I'm just so tired of being a redshirt.

A soft knock at the door interrupts my blank staring at the wall. With a sigh, I open it.

The door, not the wall. That would be silly.

Greta smiles at me. "Hi, Charlie. I was wondering if you wanted to watch a robot western tonight. I still haven't seen

01100111 01110101 01101110 01100110 01101001 01100111 01101000 01110100 00001101 00001010 at the Space Corral."

She gets it exactly right, though she has to breathe a couple times in the process. It's really nice that she's trying so hard.

I'm pretty sure she's at least reasonably fond of me. She'll help me get through this. I just need some time.

"Sure," I say. I can't wallow forever. I need to start doing normal things again. "I'll get us some pizza with cavalamitsi, and some of those donuts you like."

She smiles. She knows I'm trying hard, too.

"Our next stop is Albacore. Should we visit Oollooleeloo?" she asks.

"Why don't we just call her on the lightstream?" I suggest. "There's less possibility of a miscommunication that way."

"True. Good plan. Okay. I'll meet you back here in two hours?"

"Let's use your cabin, if you don't mind," I say. "Mine is so cramped."

She nods. "Sure! See you then!" She pauses. "I really care about you, Charlie. We're going to be okay."

"I really care about you, too," I say. "In an entirely different way than I care about Pinky. Like, light years away kind of different."

She grins. "Me too!"

She leans in and gives me a quick smooch.

As she walks away with a bounce in her step, I realize that it never occurred me to worry about that. But Greta likes to tease me.

It's nice.

I close the door. I guess I should do some work. I've been a little lax lately, but I need my job and can't afford to lose it.

There's a knock on the door and I smile. Greta must have forgotten something.

"Did you want me to bring you a Thunderstorm?" I ask as I open the door.

But it isn't Greta.

It's Pinky. And Nana.

I blink.

Yeah. That's Nana all right. She's been upgraded a little, and her cybernetic eye is now blue, but it's her all the same.

Because I'm one articulate son of a gun, I say, "Huh?"

"Got my repairs," Nana said. "Record time, too. Sometimes we're down for years."

"I thought you were dead," I blurt.

"Cyborgs don't die," Nana says. "We just become obsolete and put in a box of parts until no one can remember what we are."

"How did you get here? We're not even at a port?"

Nana says, "Pinky pulled some strings and got me approved for an in-flight docking. And she got me a one-day pass before I have to get my ass off this ship. But I wanted to see you before I go back to Mebdar IV to settle down."

This is all coming at me really fast.

"You're retiring to Mebdar IV?" I ask.

"Yep. The Mebdar IV people liked that I helped repel the cyborg attack. They're giving me VIP treatment."

"But you didn't do that," I say. "We were running away."

Pinky points at me. "Bravely. Bravely running away."

"Uh, right."

Nana shrugs. "Not the way I told it."

I laugh. Then, because I'm so happy and I don't know what else to say, I laugh some more.

Nana laughs with me, but if you've ever heard a cyborg laugh, you'll know how maniacal and disturbing it sounds. Doors open and heads poke out.

I stop laughing. Fortunately, Nana does, too.

"Well, if you get to spend the night," I say, "do you and Pinky want to come watch a movie with Greta and me tonight? It's a robot western."

I'm certain Greta won't mind me inviting them.

"Hot damn, my favorite," Nana says. "I'll bring the oil."

"I'm in, too," Pinky says. "Let's use my cabin, since there will be so many of us. It's bigger than Greta's."

I stare at her. I've been invited to Pinky's cabin. Ohmygod ohmygod ohmygod. I'm finally going to see what it's like. I expect lots of pink, and for flamingos to feature prominently.

"I'll have the pizza delivered, then," I say.

I'll never be able to carry that much myself.

"Mind if I invite Gus?" Pinky asks.

"Gus?" I'm stunned.

"Yeah. He and I have an understanding now. He's all right."

Apparently, all he needed to do to impress her was bash in a cyborg head. And apparently, all he needed to regain his sanity was to be assured that Pinky wasn't out to get him.

Actually, that makes a lot of sense.

So everybody's happy. Wow.

I mean, yay. A real yay. Not the sarcastic kind.

"Want to come to the bar with us?" Pinky asks. "Nana's going to show me some of her favorite drink recipes. I figure that might come in handy. I haven't had many cyborg guests yet, but I bet I will. We can send our food order for movie night from there."

"Sure," I agree. "You two go ahead and I'll be right there. I just need to shut off my lightstream."

"Cool," Pinky says. She does a little kick move, then a tight spin, ending in a super cool pose.

She's so damn awesome.

Inside my cabin, I turn off the lightstream. I remember that I forgot to put Greta's luck stone in my pocket after my shower. I get it out of my storage bin, and while it's open, I notice the red shirt.

I still haven't worn it. I keep saying I will. That I'll overcome my demons and wear the shirt, dodge fate, and be the master of my own destiny.

I grab the shirt and walk confidently down the corridor.

I've got friends, a space ship for a home, and a cyborg nana who's about to wreak havoc with a wildly high-stakes canasta circuit on Mebdar IV.

I'm the luckiest redshirt who ever lived.

As I pass the pulper, I stuff the shirt into it.

I may be lucky, thanks to my friends, but I'm not stupid. And I have a lot of adventures ahead of me still.

I'm ready.

MESSAGE FROM THE AUTHOR

Thank you for reading!

If you enjoyed this book and can spare a minute or two to leave a review on Amazon, I'd be grateful. It makes a big difference.

Sign up for my newsletter at www.ZenDiPietro.com to hear about new releases and sales.

I hope to hear from you!

In gratitude,

Zen DiPietro

ABOUT THE AUTHOR

Zen DiPietro is a lifelong bookworm, dreamer, and writer. Perhaps most importantly, a Browncoat Trekkie Whovian. Also red-haired, left-handed, and a vegetarian geek. Absolutely terrible at conforming. A recovering gamer, but we won't talk about that. Particular loves include badass heroines, British accents, and the smell of Band-Aids.

www.ZenDiPietro.com

OTHER WORKS

Dodging Fate Series
Dodging Fate 1
Dodging Fate 2: Extra Fateful, Uber Dodgy

Dragonfire Station Original Series
Dragonfire Station Book 1: Translucid
Dragonfire Station Book 2:Fragments
Dragonfire Station Book 3:Coalescence

Intersections (Dragonfire Station Short Stories)

Mercenary Warfare Series
Selling Out
Blood Money
Hell to Pay
Calculated Risk
Going for Broke

Chains of Command Series
New Blood

Blood and Bone
Cut to the Bone
Out for Blood

To get updates on new releases and sales, sign up for Zen's newsletter.

Printed in Dunstable, United Kingdom

66167927R00109